Call Me!

John Locke

TELEMACHUS PRESS

This book is a work of fiction. Names, characters, places and incidents are either the product of the author's imagination or are used fictitiously. Any resemblance to actual persons, living or dead, or to actual events or locales is entirely coincidental.

CALL ME!

Cover Designed by: Telemachus Press, LLC
Cover Art :
Copyright © istockphoto 162619 (Foster)
Copyright © istockphoto 4713823 (Lukic)
Copyright © istockphoto 18053195 (Petolea)

Telemachus Press, LLC
http://www.telemachuspress.com

Visit the author website:
http://www.DonovanCreed.com

ISBN: 978-1-937698-55-3

Printed in the United States of America

10 9 8 7 6 5 4 3 2 1

John Locke

New York Times Best Selling Author
#1 Best Selling Author on Amazon Kindle

Donovan Creed Series:

Lethal People
Lethal Experiment
Saving Rachel
Now & Then
Wish List
A Girl Like You
Vegas Moon
The Love You Crave
Maybe
Callie's Last Dance
Because We Can!

Emmett Love Series:

Follow the Stone
Don't Poke the Bear!
Emmett & Gentry
Goodbye, Enorma

Dani Ripper Series:

Call Me!
Promise You Won't Tell?
Teacher, Teacher

Dr. Gideon Box Series:

Bad Doctor
Box
Outside the Box

Other:

Kill Jill
Casting Call

Young Adult:

A Kiss for Luck (Kindle Only)

Non-Fiction:

How I Sold 1 Million eBooks in 5 Months!

Call Me!

Chapter 1

THURSDAY

"IT'S HARD TO look dignified with a dick in your mouth."

"*Excuse* me?"

My new client, Carter Teague, needs to understand I'm a decoy, not a hooker. In other words, I'm not going to have sex with her boyfriend.

"Fiancé," she says.

"Whatever. I'll get him in my hotel room, and you can walk in on us from the adjoining room. But we won't actually be naked."

Carter looks exasperated. "He could come up with a million excuses if you're dressed. But if I walk in and you're both naked, what's he going to say?"

She looks around my office.

I know what that means.

She's noting the disarray. The fact I don't have a secretary. And do have a bag of trash that's overdue for the garbage. She checks my business card for the second time and sees my name, Dani Ripper, is not raised or embossed. She rightfully assumes a female private eye in Cincinnati, Ohio, rarely gets the big clients.

She knows I need the money.

"What if I sweeten the pot?" she says.

"I'm not a hooker, Ms. Teague."

"No, of course not!" Carter says, shaking her head. "I'm sorry. I didn't mean to imply—"

I wave her off. "It's okay. I just want to be clear."

There are two faux leather chairs across from my desk. Carter's sitting in the one closest to the door. She's thirty. Dressing younger, but thirty, which makes her six years older than me.

I'd stake my life on it.

Her shoulder-length hair is russet, with amber highlights, if you care about such things. I do, and make a note to ask who does her hair, though it's probably a week's pay for me. I did happen to notice her Casadei back-zip wedge sandals when she entered, though they're currently hidden by the desk. The part of her I *can* see is wearing an off-shoulder leopard tunic, with bracelets that match my annual house payment. She exudes wealth, and proves it by saying, "I'll pay you two thousand plus expenses."

"For two thousand you could hire the best hooker in town."

"This isn't about sex, Ms. Ripper. I don't want to catch him *cheating*, I just need to know if he *would*. There's a lot at

2

stake here. The wedding *alone* will cost my father a quarter million."

Two grand means I get to keep driving my car.

"Bra and panties?" I offer.

"Three thousand," she says. "All cash."

"In advance?"

"If you wish."

I wince, thinking about it.

"Maybe I could lose the bra. But my panties aren't negotiable."

"Five thousand dollars!" she calls out with all the enthusiasm of a trophy wife at a charity auction. "All cash. In advance." She pauses, then says, "My final offer."

I bite my lip.

"Take it or leave it," she says.

"No photos," I say.

"*What?* Why not?"

"Are you *serious?*"

Carter sighs. "Deal."

Her fiancé's name is Joe Fagin. He's thirty-two. We review his photos together. She wants to set it up for tomorrow night at the Brundage Hotel in Louisville, where he has dinner reservations at Simon Claire's at seven-fifteen.

"Have you ever been there?" I ask.

"No."

"The restaurant's on the second floor. There's an open area, then the bar."

"Perfect."

"Who's Joe meeting for dinner?"

"Computer geeks, trying to raise money."

3

"Joe's a venture capitalist?"

"He thinks so, but my father suspects he can't fund his deals. Mind you, there's no evidence of that."

"Do you know if they have plans for after dinner?"

"Joe Fagin hanging out with computer geeks?" she laughs. "He's not the type. You'll see. I expect he'll lose them after dinner, probably hit the Brundage bar."

"Or catch a cab somewhere more exciting."

She frowns. "That could mess things up."

"I'll work it out."

"I admire your confidence."

"I'm confident I can get his attention. Enticing him to come to my room is something entirely different."

"You'll try your best?"

"Of course. But if he doesn't take the bait..."

"Then we live happily ever after."

"You'd consider him faithful if I can't seduce him in a single encounter?"

"Absolutely." She notes my puzzled expression and says, "I mean, look at you!"

I can't look at me, but she does. In fact, she studies me so deliberately it makes me uncomfortable.

She says, "If he can resist you, I'll marry him. If not, I'll be heartbroken, but better off."

She opens her purse and removes a bundle of hundreds wrapped in a Union City Bank paper band.

"That's five," she says.

To her amusement, I spread the bills across my desktop and run a counterfeit money pen over them. When I'm satisfied they're real, she reaches in her purse and removes another bundle of equal size and denomination, and peels five bills from that one.

"Expenses," she says.

I run the pen over those, as well.

As I watch her leave my office, I recall how she entered it thirty minutes earlier. She knocked on my door, tentatively. I told her to come in. When she did, she looked at me and her eyes widened.

That was the first thing I noticed, her eyes. I'd never seen harlequin-green eyes before.

"Wow," she said.

"Wow?"

"You're beautiful."

"Thanks," I said. "That's quite a compliment, coming from you."

And it was, because Carter Teague's a knockout. As a woman, I'm allowed to say that. I'm allowed to notice, too. It's funny how we can get away with looking at, and even touching, other women. I wasn't interested in touching her boobs, of course, but I could've said something like, "Are those real? No? Oh, my God, they're *spectacular*! May I?" Then I could've reached out and touched them. She would've been embarrassed, but she'd have allowed it. If a man tried that, he'd find himself in an orange jumpsuit before the noon whistle signals lunch at county.

Funny, that.

I think she caught me looking at her boobs just then, because she suddenly averted her eyes and pretended to glance out my office window. She did that a few seconds, then turned back and focused her eyes on mine.

"You're Ms. Ripper?" she said.

"Please. Call me Dani. And you're?"

"Carter Teague."

"Great name," I said.

"Thanks."

We were both quiet a moment.

"Um...you're staring," I said.

"Oh. Sorry!"

"No problem. I'm flattered. I think."

She wasn't blushing, more like flushed. And staring again.

"You're married?" she said.

"Yes."

"Happily?"

How does any married woman answer that question? Depends on the hour, the day, the time of month...

"I like to think so," I say. "How can I help you?"

She removed my business card from the card holder on my desk and held it between her perfectly manicured thumb and index finger.

"You're a private investigator?" she said.

"I am."

"I was told you're a decoy."

"By whom?"

"I heard my father talking to someone. He's a divorce attorney."

"Here?"

"No. Cleveland."

"And he's heard of *me*?"

"He was telling someone you're the best in the business."

"I've done some decoy work. Not locally."

"This would be in Louisville, not Cincinnati."

I nodded. She explained what she wanted, and how she planned to walk in on her fiancé and me while having sex, and I explained how I don't actually have sex with the husbands or boyfriends, and—wait. I'm wasting your time. You're caught up. Let's move along.

Chapter 2

TWO THINGS HAVE happened. Carter Teague has left the building, and I've got another decoy job.

The sign on the door says *Dani Ripper, Private Investigator*. As does the ad in the phone book. The business cards. The social media listings all over the internet.

Dani Ripper, Private Investigator.

The word "decoy" cannot be found associated with my name, but that's the work I get.

I'm not shocked, there are reasons I'm not on the short list for the big PI jobs. First, I'm a woman.

I don't mean it the way you think.

What I mean is most clients think this type of work involves physical encounters with seamy, bent-nosed characters. Clients are conditioned to expect a PI who'll hang a brute on a meat hook and beat the shit out of him with a tire iron to find out where he hid the jewels. They tend to view me as tight jeans, five-inch heels, and a kick-ass halter.

I'm the first to admit I'm not tough.

I don't grunt, sweat, or smell. I know some basic moves, but I'm more at home on a dance floor than a kick boxing ring. In short, I don't look the part. Which is funny, since ninety-nine percent of the job involves computer and camera work, and sitting in cars waiting for people to exit homes, hotels or businesses. Less than one percent involves physical contact.

The second reason I don't get much PI business is I've never had a high-profile case. In this business one high profile case will feed you a lifetime of clients.

Let me amend that statement: I *have* had a high-profile case. I just didn't solve it. And that's the third reason I don't get much PI business.

I scoop Carter's cash off my desk and stuff it in my shoulder tote. I'm a Choo girl on a Kors budget, which is to say I'll splurge to a point when I get a windfall.

Which isn't often.

Today's a windfall, but I've already earmarked Carter's cash for practical things, like catching up on my car payments. And the mortgage. I'll also put a grand toward my step-son's college fund. Buy some groceries and household cleaning supplies. And...wait. I might have enough left to splurge. Tomorrow I'll buy a nice gift for best friend Sophie Alexander, whose birthday happens to be today. This morning Sophie was the proud recipient of a whimsical email card and an invitation to a birthday lunch on Tuesday. Thanks to Carter Teague, Sophie's lunch has been upgraded to dinner and a bracelet. I'll get her something trendy, but tasteful.

So the clothes, jewelry, fancy cars, mansions, yachts and such will be placed on hold till I finally crack a high-profile case. And that's fine, since I suspect it's more fun to dream about exquisite material things than it is to insure and maintain them. While I admit to owning a few signature pieces, like my Gucci watch (a gift from Sophie) I'm not a clothes whore. I'd much rather have a fond vacation memory than a pair of designer pumps.

With ninety minutes to kill before my lunch appointment with Vicky Stringfellow, I go back to what I was doing before Carter showered me with cash, which happens to be the same thing I always do when I have time on my hands.

Check my emails.

It's not what you think.

I check emails the same way you do, and read and answer them the same way you do. But, unlike you, I'm checking to see if my alerts have been triggered. I use all the alert programs, seeking hits to variations on the phrase that haunts my days and nights.

A quick scan shows no recent hits. But most of my alerts are updated every twenty-four hours, so I go to Google and type the word *cherrystones*.

167,000 entries.

I scan the first dozen pages, as always, but can't find what I want. I narrow the search by typing *Are your nipples like cherrystones?*

That phrase turns up 19,200 entries, but none on the first dozen pages contain the exact wording. So I try *nipples like cherrystones.*

And get 11,200,000 entries.

Crazy, right?

But as I scan the first dozen pages of this search, I find two references. One on a dating site, another in a chat room.

The dating site would be an uncharacteristic departure for my target, but my pulse quickens, as it always does, whenever these (or similar) words are typed in a chat room that underage girls are likely to frequent. I copy the link into my browser, click it, and learn it requires an annual credit card payment of nineteen dollars.

I sigh.

That brings my total to fourteen paid sites and forty-seven free ones. That's sixty-one sites if my math skills haven't deserted me. I check each of these sites at least once a week. Do I have that much time to spare?

No. But what am I going to do?

I'm obsessed.

I create a new email account and sign up with a unique name and password, and record the information in my notebook. Most chat room sites are so simple to navigate it only takes a minute to catch the groove, and this one's no different.

The boy/man/pervert? who made the reference is listed as *SeanInPain*, and his current status is *Offline*. There's no photo, but his avatar—consisting of the words *Bad Boy* scrawled in black ink with red blood dripping down the letters—is twisted enough to attract the twelve to fifteen-year-old female demographic my target seeks: those who think they want a brooding, dangerous, slightly-older guy.

I click his profile and roll my eyes. He claims to be from *Everywhere*. His age is described as *Old Soul*. His likes are *Let's just say you couldn't handle it!* His dislikes are *Whiny girls who run to mommy.*

A cold chill runs through my body. *SeanInPain* is a prime candidate!

I scroll his recent posts till I find the reference, written nineteen hours ago: *I saw my sister naked in the shower just now. Her breasts are small, the exact size of the silicone inserts I found in her underwear drawer last week. On the box they claim to increase your bra size by 1.5 cups. But if you lay them on a table, they're pretty damn flat. Sorry guys. My sister's tits are flat and unattractive. But her nipples are hard, like cherrystones. More on this soon.*

Asshole.

Not because he sneaks in the bathroom to spy on his sister, and not because he reports her nudity to the world. Sure, spying on your sister is over-the-top creepy, and this little shit has obviously got twenty-to-life issues.

But that's not what makes him an asshole.

What makes him an asshole is he cost me nineteen bucks and he's not the guy. *SeanInPain* is someone else's pervert. He's my guy ten years ago. But my pervert is older. Late twenties, I think. Used to call himself *ManChild*. When he writes the phrase in a chat room, it won't be an eye-witness report on his sister's cleavage. It'll be a question, asked by a grown man to a teenage girl between the ages of twelve and fifteen. And what he'll ask is, *Are your nipples like cherrystones? Are they hard and firm? Are they as hard and firm as the erection in my pants?*

There's more, of course, but I'll spare you the details. Just thinking about it makes me want to take a shower.

Chapter 3

VICKY STRINGFELLOW AND I greet each other the way we've been socially conditioned to greet other women: by raising our voices an octave, gushing with fake enthusiasm, and finding something about the other to compliment. She chooses my figure, I choose her eyes. Since I called the meeting, social etiquette requires me to throw in an extra compliment, so I say, "Vicky, where on earth did you find that killer top?"

She smiles. "You really like it?"

"I *love* it!"

"Believe it or not, I found it at Leversons."

We chitchat about where Leversons is located, and who I should ask for when I check it out. As we talk, we appraise each other the way we've been conditioned all our lives to appraise other women: by noting their flaws.

I'm well aware of mine, but if you want that information you'll have to ask Vicky. As for hers, I'm not overly critical, and I want very much to like her, so I'll just say she's a little overweight, and could use some help with hair and makeup. On the other hand, she's intelligent, pleasant, and available.

"How long have you been divorced?" I say.

I didn't just blurt that out, we're actually twenty minutes into the conversation at this point, and the waiter has just brought our salads, and fussed over us with offers of fresh-ground pepper and hand-grated cheese.

Vicky tells me what I need to know about her and Charles: they broke up two years ago, no kids, she teaches fourth grade at a private school, and has her own townhome in Willoughby Commons. She's dated several men, but nothing clicked because she wasn't ready to begin a new relationship.

Till now.

As she talks, I mentally tick each item with a checkmark on my list. Vicky's not bitter or needy. She's independent, self-sustaining, and ready to move on with her life.

"So..." she says, and I know we've come to the tricky part.

"Yes?"

"Tell me about this professor you've found for me."

"He teaches at Clifton State."

She arches her eyebrows. In a good way. But waits for me to continue.

"His name's Ben Davis," I say. "He's thirty-eight."

15

She lifts her chin slightly, purses her lips. I know what she's thinking.

Vicky Davis.

Her eyes widen the slightest bit. I wouldn't have noticed had I not been studying her so closely. But her eyes tell me Vicky likes the sound of her name with Ben's, a critical issue, since she's still using her married name.

"How long have you known Ben?" she asks.

"Seven years."

"And you *still* think he's a good guy?"

She laughs.

I laugh.

"He's a *great* guy," I say. "A true gentleman. The smartest man I know."

She frowns. "If he's that great, why aren't *you* dating him?"

I bite my bottom lip. "I'm married."

She instinctively looks at my left hand.

"You're not wearing a ring."

"It's complicated."

Vicky nods, slowly. She wants to pursue the conversation, but doesn't want to intrude, or appear too nosey this early in our relationship. Steering the conversation back to Ben, she says, "How many times has the good professor been married?"

"Twice."

"Oh," she says, suddenly deflated. She frowns.

"It's not as bad as it sounds," I say.

"Tell me why."

"Well, he's only been divorced once."

She cocks her head. "One of his wives passed away?"

My turn to frown. I have to word this carefully. This is the part where I always lose them. I rehearsed it in my head ten times, but it should have been twenty, because the right words aren't coming.

Vicky says, "Did one of his wives die?"

"Not exactly."

She frowns again. At the pace she's frowning, I wonder how long it'll take her face to develop worry lines.

"I'm afraid I don't understand," Vicky says. "He's been married twice, divorced once, and one of his wives hasn't passed away. Is this a riddle?"

"It *can* be."

"Excuse me?"

"Here's the thing. He's still married."

"*What?*" She jumps to her feet.

"Wait. It's not what you think. Please. Sit down."

She frowns again. Vicky's quite angry, but we're in a public place and people are staring at us. Common courtesy dictates she at least offer to split the check. She knows this, and starts fumbling around in her purse.

"Vicky," I say, "please. Let me explain."

She sighs, and reclaims her seat.

"I don't appreciate your wasting my time like this," she says. "You can't possibly think I'd be interested in dating a married man."

I hold up my hand. "Ordinarily I wouldn't. But this guy's special. You can get to know him on Mondays and Tuesdays."

"He's *married*, Dani. That's a deal-breaker."

"Here's the thing," I say.

"Yes?"

"He's married to me."

"*What?*"

"Ben's my husband. And I swear, he's a wonderful man."

She looks around. "Are there cameras in here? Am I being punked?"

"No, of course not."

"Then...what? Are you insane?"

"Not clinically. I don't think. Well, maybe."

Vicky places a twenty on the table by her untouched salad. "This should more than cover my lunch," she says. She stands, walks about twenty feet, turns, and comes back to the table.

"Does Ben know you're shopping him around?"

"No. It would kill him if he found out."

Her eyes become slits. "Are you telling me he doesn't even know you're planning to leave him?"

I look down at my salad.

She says, "How long have you been cheating on him?"

I say nothing, though I've never cheated on Ben.

"When are you planning to tell him?"

"I won't leave him till I know he's got a better woman than me in his life."

She frowns for a record fifth time. "No offense," she says, "but I don't think it'll take much of a woman to be an improvement."

I flash a hopeful smile. "Does that mean you're willing to meet him?"

She spins around and starts walking away, swiftly.
I holler, "We could have you over for dinner!"

Chapter 4

I'M HOME NOW, meaning I'm in the two-story townhome I share with my husband, Ben Davis. Ben's not home yet. It's Thursday, and he's got a class from four to five. I'm in the kitchen, putting up the groceries I just unloaded from the car. Ben occupies the bedroom on the first floor, I sleep upstairs.

Ben's a wonderful man. Anyone will tell you that. What they won't tell you is I don't deserve him.

But it's true, I don't.

He treats me like a princess, I treat him like a friend. I've thought about leaving him many times, but love him far too much to let him be alone. Also, I don't want him to go through a second bad divorce. I keep thinking if I can get him involved with a nice woman who'll put out for him regularly, Ben might fall in love with her and ask *me* for a divorce. Barring that, if I can get him infatuated with another woman, we could sit down and have a divorce discussion. Of course I could always hire a woman to do what I do: lure Ben to her motel room, catch him cheating, throw a fit and demand a divorce.

But I would never do that to Ben. Sure, I do it all the time for other women, divorce attorneys, private investigators, free-lance journalists, and political strategists. But that's my job.

I know what you're thinking: calling it my job doesn't make it right.

True.

But a job's a job, and this one pays the bills. You see, I pay my own way in the marriage, which means half the mortgage, half the utilities, half the groceries, and so forth. I make my own car payment, buy my own clothes. I even kick in some extra money to help with Ben's son. I do this because I don't have the heart to take, take, take from Ben, while giving nothing in return.

By "nothing," I mean sex.

When I stopped being sexually available for him, we had a discussion. It took me a bucket of tears and lots of prodding on his part before I finally admitted I didn't find him attractive "in that way" anymore. I begged him to forgive me for that. He did, instantly, and asked me to stay with him anyway. I told him it wouldn't be right. I'd make him miserable. Told him he deserved better. He said he'd rather be miserable with me than happy with someone else.

He meant it better than it sounds. Although Ben's a professor, and words are his tools, communication isn't his strong suit. He often says meaningful things that get lost in the translation. It's a Ben thing. You wouldn't understand. Unless you knew him better.

At any rate, when he asked me to stay with him I said, "The least I can do is pay half the expenses."

He wouldn't hear of it, but I insisted.

"Any other demands?" he said.

"I want two nights a week for myself."

"Excuse me?"

"Two nights to myself. Each week."

"What, you want me to stay in a hotel?"

"No. I want to leave the house, leave this life, two nights a week."

"Sounds like you've thought this all out."

"Actually, it just now came to me."

"There's another man," he said.

"No."

"No?"

"I promise."

"What will you do every week on these two nights?"

"Different things. But the other five nights I'll be available for you."

"But not *sexually* available."

"Not sexually, no."

"Define available," he said.

"When I'm not working a case I'll buy groceries, cook dinner, go out with you to your functions and fund-raisers, or to dinner, plays, movies, whatever. I'll run errands, help you entertain friends and colleagues. I'll help you grade papers. I'll—"

"I get the point," he said. "And I assume on these two nights a week you'll be available to have sex with other men?"

I looked him in the eyes. "Ben, I'm not looking for another man."

"But if one happens to show up? One you can't resist?"

"If that happens, we'll have another discussion."

"Before you date him?"

"Yes."

"Promise?"

"I won't cheat on you. I promise."

Ben didn't know about my decoy work back then and still doesn't know I occasionally get paid to lure strange men to hotel rooms. Ben might consider this dating, but I have no problem separating my decoy work from my social life.

"Which nights?" Ben said.

"You pick."

"Monday and Tuesday. That gives us the weekends."

"Done."

He said, "I believe you."

"Thank you."

"If you wanted the weekends, I'd know you had someone else."

"Because someone else would demand my weekends?"

"Exactly."

"You can live like this? Having me as a roommate instead of a wife?"

"I'll manage."

"How?"

"After the third year of marriage, twenty-five percent of married couples sleep in separate bedrooms."

"They keep statistics on those sorts of things?"

"They do. And most wives want less sex with their husbands every year, especially after they've had kids. Eventually, sexual frequency for married couples is statistically nonexistent."

"But for us it's already nonexistent."

"But we get along great," he said. "And you gave me three wonderful years of sexual memories."

I smiled. "Those were fun times. But, the two nights I'm gone every week from now on?"

"What about them?"

"I don't want to talk about them."

He pauses.

"Fine," he says.

"Really?"

"I won't ask what you do if you don't ask what I do."

We laughed and shook hands on it, like two moguls closing a business deal.

Chapter 5

"WHAT ABOUT BIRTHDAYS?" Ben said.

"Birthdays?"

"I think it's customary for wives to give their husbands a blowjob on birthdays, and have sex on Valentine's and anniversaries."

I frowned. "Maybe this isn't going to work out."

"Forget the BJ's. How about sex? Three days a year. What do you think?"

I wonder why it's so hard for me to accommodate him. Ben's a handsome, wonderful man who adores me. This is the man who saved my life by loving me when I was in the depths of despair. This is a man who's willing to live under the same roof without intimacy, a man who's capable of trusting his wife to be gone two days a week without requiring any explanation for her actions or whereabouts.

Still, I knew I couldn't do Valentine's Day. That's a day for lovers.

He looked at me with hope in his eyes.

It was pitiful.

"How about a hand job?" I said, enthusiastically.

He frowned and turned away.

"I'll give you the two nights each week," he said, "and let you split the marital expenses. But your business is touch and go, so I hope you'll allow me to pay the bills if you ever find yourself short."

"If that happens, I'll pay you back as soon as I can."

He nodded, still facing away.

"Ben?"

"Yeah?"

"I do love you," I said.

"I know."

"Ben?"

"Yeah?"

I paused.

He turned to face me.

"I'll do the sex thing, twice a year. Your birthday and our wedding anniversary."

He laughed. "The sex *thing?*"

"Poor choice of words," I said, expecting him to make a nasty remark and tell me to kiss off. But he surprised me.

"I'll take it," he said. "Sex, twice a year."

I nodded.

"You promise?"

"Yes." Then added, "As long as we're living together."

He studied my face a moment, then said, "I can live with that."

And that's how it's been for the past year. Every Monday after breakfast I drive somewhere.

Usually Nashville.

And every Wednesday I drive home.

I check my watch. Four-thirty. Ben will call shortly after five to let me know if he wants to go out for dinner and drinks or have me whip something up. I'm not a great cook, but compared to his first wife, Ben says I'm Julia Child.

Ben and Erica had a terrible marriage and a worse breakup. There are always two sides to these stories, but the one I heard and believe is Erica was obsessed with having a baby. So once a week for months (while I was an innocent fourteen-year-old junior high school student), Ben Davis dutifully ejaculated his sperm into donor vials instead of his wife. This, because Erica's fertility doctor determined Ben's sperm count was low, and had mobility issues. Erica and her doctor decreed Ben should refrain from any activity that offers sexual relief outside the fertility clinic, in order to create the strongest possible sperm count.

But it didn't help.

Ben's inability to get his wife pregnant led to arguments during which he complained about their sex life and she ridiculed him for being less than a real man. When he stopped going to the fertility clinic she never slept with him again. For three years Ben ignored rumors she was cheating, but that changed when she turned up pregnant with Tuck Wilson's baby. Tuck's wife, Carol, discovered the affair, bought a megaphone, and dogged Erica in public places announcing, "Erica Davis is cheating on her husband with Tuck Wilson, her tennis instructor!"

At Fairwick Gym, Carol yelled, "The woman in the yellow tank top with the fake boobs is Erica Davis. She's having an affair with my husband, Tuck Wilson. I have two babies at home. What kind of home-wrecking bitch would do that?"

When she brought out the megaphone and called Erica a "dick-breathed whore" in the Glen Aden Mall in downtown Cincinnati, Carol was arrested, and the affair became public knowledge. The "Megaphone Mama" became an internet sensation, and Ben and Erica's marriage was fodder for talk show hosts all over the world. The publicity proved too embarrassing for Ben's employer, Riverton College, and Ben found himself without a job. This, plus Erica's complete lack of remorse for the affair, brought the marriage to a swift end.

Shortly thereafter, Erica lost Tuck's baby. But the crazy twist is, she and Ben had prepaid for six additional treatments, and she used Ben's frozen sperm without his knowledge. Wouldn't you know it? The fifth treatment worked, and Ben's former wife was with child.

His child.

Erica hoped for a reconciliation, but Ben was having none of it.

What no one knew at the time, he had his eye on someone else.

Me.

As I said, I met Ben during a particularly difficult time in my life. By then I was seventeen, he was thirty-one. I'd been in hiding for two years, and private tutors helped me get my high school equivalency. My mother hoped I'd go to college, but I was unable to face the world.

We were living in Cincinnati, looking for a college tutor.

Ben was a recently divorced man, reeling from an internationally publicized breakup. He was also an unemployed college professor who had placed ads all over town looking for work tutoring students. My mom saw the ad, gave him a call, and he became my college tutor.

A year later, he became my husband.

Chapter 6

NOW THAT THE groceries are put away, I pop the lid on a diet soda and bring it upstairs. I don't have a formal office up here like Ben has on the first floor, but what I have works for me. I'll give you a quick tour if you like, but try not to blink.

This open area at the top of the stairs, overlooking the den, is what passes for my office. You'll notice the windows on the far side offer a view of the front yard. On this side, if you look over the railing, you'll see our back yard through the sliding glass doors of the den. It's about the size of a postage stamp, so there's not much labor required to keep it tidy.

Yes, my office area is small. Room only for a desk and chair, but what else do I need? I've got a laptop, printer, and cell phone charger on the desk, supplies in the drawers.

Come, I'll show you the rest of the upstairs.

It's a mere ten steps from my desk to the door of my bedroom. There's my Queen-size bed and the single night stand and lamp. You'll note the huge dresser on the opposite wall, and the thirty-six inch TV atop it.

Yes, I could afford a larger TV, but I only watch to fall asleep, so I'm quite content. Yes, I've got cable. No, I don't have HD. Yes, I know the closets are small. But there are two of them, and remember, the dresser's ji-normous.

My cell phone is ringing, so I'll wrap this up. The window overlooks the driveway. The open door leads to the bathroom...and that's about it.

Caller ID is coming up blank, so I answer the phone cheerfully.

"Dani Ripper, how can I help you?"

"I think my husband's cheating."

"If you think he is, he probably is. Want me to find out for sure?"

"I reckon so."

"That's the spirit!"

I get to my desk, get out a legal pad and pen and say, "What's your name?"

"Jeredith Baker."

"And how old are you, Ms. Baker?"

"What difference does that make?"

"I'm building a profile. I'm not on the clock yet, so anything you tell me now will save you money later."

"I don't have much money."

"Hey, me either!" I say, "and you know why? Because my prices are so reasonable! But I'm very good at my job, and I'll get you a fast result."

"Well, you sound like a go-getter."

"Thanks. How old are you, Jeredith?"

"Sixty-two."

I shake my head. She's probably mistaken about her husband cheating. Still, I can charge her for my time, knowing she'll be even happier if her husband turns out to be faithful.

"What's your husband's name?"

"Burt."

"Burt Baker?"

"Yep."

"And how old is Burt?"

"Sixty-six."

A thought crosses my mind.

"Is Burt taking medication for erectile dysfunction?" I ask.

"Is that the little blue pill?"

"Yes. But there are other colors for similar medications."

"He takes a lot of medicine, but probably not that type. Burt doesn't dance much."

"Excuse me?"

"In the commercials on TV they always show people dancing after taking those blue pills. And smiling. They take the pill, they dance, they smile, they hold hands. Does that sound like Burt to you?"

I can't believe I'm participating in this conversation. Shows how badly I want to do some real PI work.

"So, Burt doesn't dance?" I say.

"No ma'am, nor smile much, neither."

We go back and forth like that awhile, and I start building a profile. I'm surprised to learn Burt spends hours at a time online, so I tell Jeredith I'd like to have a look at his computer.

"Wednesday at one o'clock," she says. "He always leaves the house at noon on Wednesday, and stays gone till night time."

"Do you ask where he goes?"

"Of course. But he tells me to shut my trap and mind my own business."

I frown. Already I don't like Burt. I tell her I'll see her on Wednesday. Then I call Dillon.

"Captain Spaceship," he says.

"Dillon, it's me, Dani."

"I want to be called Captain Spaceship."

"That doesn't make sense."

"Still, it's what I want."

I sigh. It's not easy dealing with teenage computer nerds.

"How about I call you CS?"

"Are you *crazy*?"

"CS. Captain Spaceship."

"CS stands for cock sucker."

"Oh. Sorry."

"Jeez, Dani."

"Look. I'll make you a deal. I won't call you Captain Spaceship and you don't have to call me Princess Washing Machine. The thing is I've got a job for you. If you don't want it, I'll do it myself."

His laugh sounds like the braying of an asthmatic donkey. And once it starts, like now, it goes on and on. When it finally ends he says, "Are my *ears* functioning correctly? Did I hear you say you'll do it *yourself?* You couldn't find a jpeg in a music file!"

"Dillon, either take the job or hang up. If you hang up, I'll never call again."

"When and where?"

I tell him.

"How much?"

"Sixty."

"Thousand?"

"Dollars, Dillon. Sixty dollars."

"What's the job?"

"We're hacking a sixty-six-year-old man's computer, on site. Think you're up to it?"

He laughs. "I should be arrested for stealing your money."

"That's the spirit," I say.

Chapter 7

AFTER ENDING THE call with Dillon I log onto my laptop and check for updates.

BillInNeed claims to have hooked up with a virgin. Of course he has. Just like I hooked up with Brad Pitt last night. *FingerSniffer* challenges "all underage whores" to send him "nekkid pix," and *StickyRicky* has opened a discussion thread that asks, "What's the wildest thing you've done, in exactly five words?" The post is only twenty minutes old but he's already logged twenty-two responses. I read them with mild interest, because it's not easy to express yourself in exactly five words.

One surprises me.

SimonHymen, male, 15, posted: "Had sex with girlfriend's father."

Eew.

SeanInPain's new post should stir things up among the dregs of humanity: *I have dirty thoughts about my sister. She's fifteen and hot! I want to drug her and do vile things. Tell me what to do to her. Details, please.*

My cell phone rings again.

"Hi, honey," Ben says. "Want to go out tonight?"

"I'm up for a beer and appetizer," I say.

"How about Carson's?"

"Carson's is cocktails, not beer. Are we celebrating something?"

"My birthday."

I do the math in my head. "That's in three months."

He laughs. "Can't blame a guy for trying."

At Carson's, over drinks, I learn he wants me to give up my Tuesday.

"I can't."

"It wouldn't be the whole day," he says, "just Tuesday night."

"Why?"

"I want us to take an old friend of mine out to dinner."

The thing is I can accommodate him, since I haven't called Sophie to switch our Tuesday lunch to dinner yet.

"It'd mean a lot to me," he says.

"What's so important about this friend?"

"It's Roy Burroughs."

"Who's that?"

"My college roommate."

I shake my head. "You guys would have much more fun without me. You can go out drinking, talk dirty, swap lies."

He frowns. "You think that's what guys do?"

"When you're not belching, scratching, or passing gas."

"Funny."

"Seriously. You could take him to a titty bar, get a lap dance."

He nods. "Okay. Forget it."

Now I feel bad. Ben asks for so little. Dinner with his old friend is the least I can do.

"What time?" I say.

He looks at me with interest. "When could you be back?"

"Six o'clock."

"Thanks, Dani."

"Will Roy's wife be joining us?"

"He's not married."

We're quiet a while. Then I ask, "How come you never talk about this guy?"

"I hate his guts."

"You'll note the confused look on my face," I say.

"All through school he was the biggest jerk," Ben says. "Whatever I did, he had to top it. He had the money, the car, the grades, the girlfriends."

"He intimidated you."

"He was popular. A great athlete."

"He lives here? In town?"

"Miami. He's coming in town to close a big real estate deal. Wants to meet us for dinner, so he can rub his success in my face."

"Why didn't you say you were busy?"

"Because I've got *you*."

"Confused look on my face again."

"When he sees you, he'll shit his pants!"

"He will? What a charmer! Silly me, willing to settle for a handshake."

"I'm serious. You're going to blow him away."

"Thanks for adding the last word in the sentence."

"You're funny tonight."

"But on Tuesday I'm what, your trophy?"

"In a manner of speaking."

He looks at me. "Roy doesn't have to know how things really are between us. It'll be the first time in my life I actually beat him at something."

"Can you hear how sad that makes you sound?"

"I'll give you an extra day next week," he says.

"Sunday or Wednesday?"

"Your choice."

"Sunday."

"Thanks, Dani. I know it sounds perverse, but it would mean a lot to me."

"I'll try not to disappoint you."

After the waiter takes our order we talk about *ManChild*. Ben says I haven't spoken about him for a while, and was curious if I was still hunting him. I tell him *ManChild* frustrates me like Roy frustrates him, but I won't give up. He says he's proud of me for sticking with it.

While eating, we talk like married people. He wants to know if I'll stay home tomorrow so the air conditioner guy can do the six-month maintenance. I can, and remind him the pest control guy is scheduled for Tuesday morning. Ben's got that covered. We talk about our bills, then he yawns and says he couldn't sleep last night because his back flared up.

"You should have called me," I say.

"Why?"

"I would've rubbed your back."

"You were in bed."

"Next time, call me. If you're in pain, I want to help."

"Thanks. That's sweet of you to say."

"I mean it. I'll rub your back tonight, before you go to bed."

He shows me a weak smile. "I'll be fine," he says.

I know what that's about. He's told me before. In the early days, the massages were sensual, a romantic prelude to sex. Now, any touching beyond a respectful hug or kiss is painful to him, because it brings back memories of how things used to be, and can never be again.

The first time he tried to explain it, I said, "You're better off without me."

"No," he said. "I need you in my life."

"Can you explain that?" I said. "Because it sounds like everything I do reminds you I've turned into a frigid, uncaring wife."

He laughed.

Then I said, "Wait. I just made that all about me, didn't I."

He smiled. "You've seen those vodka bottles with a giant orange inside?"

"Yes! How do they *do* that?"

"Not important. The point I'm making, the only way to get the orange out is to crush it, or break the bottle."

"So?"

"Our relationship is like the orange in the vodka bottle."

I think about that. Then say, "I have no idea what you're talking about."

"I'm the bottle, and you're the orange in my life. I'm here to protect you from the outside world, and you're here to complete me. You could leave, but you'd be vulnerable, and I'd be empty inside. You could leave, but it would destroy what we have together."

"But what we have *sucks!*"

"Not true. Only the lack of intimacy sucks. And the two days you spend away from me doing God knows what. Everything else adds up to a great marriage."

"But those are huge issues!"

"Two issues, and yes, I agree they're huge. But you're worth it."

"You just haven't met the right woman yet."

"And don't want to."

"Why not?"

"You've heard the expression apples and oranges? Compared to you, other women are apples."

"That's ridiculous. You're a hell of a catch. I could find you a dozen oranges in the space of a day."

"Perhaps you could," he said. "But none like you."

"You need to replace me with a better orange, Ben."

"There *are* no better oranges, Dani."

Chapter 8

FRIDAY

THE BAD NEWS is the air conditioning guy was two hours late showing up this morning. The good news is it took less than an hour to replace the filters and check everything out.

It's noon. I'm in Neiman's.

The jewelry department is...over there. But I'm here...in handbags. I try to make my legs move toward jewelry, where Sophie's trendy-but-tasteful birthday bracelet is patiently waiting in a case for me to discover.

But I'm not moving in that direction. I want to, but my legs are stuck in Gucci quicksand!

My plan had been simple. I intended to enter the front door and walk purposefully, eyes forward, directly past beauty, fragrances, fashion accessories, shoes, and handbags.

In jewelry, as opposed to *fine* jewelry, I'd locate Sophie's bracelet in a non-lighted glass case.

Things were going great until a leather-scented tractor beam pulled me off course. I don't understand quantum physics, but I do know there's something magic about the scent of hand-tooled leather, and the urgency that comes with certain knowledge a shipment of designer handbags has recently been placed on display.

"No, Dani. No, Dani. No, Dani," I say loudly enough that a nearby child darts behind her mother to keep a safe distance from the crazy lady. But in my head I'm saying, *a good friend would do a quick walkthrough to let Sophie know what's arrived.* And a good friend *would*, because everything on these shelves is within Sophie's budget. Mine is...well, my budget's a zip code away.

I get about three feet before my eyes begin tracking the movements of a Gucci handbag heading toward me, held for my viewing pleasure by a young, foreign salesperson with a sinful smile. I don't see him smile, but he must be smiling because my eyes are transfixed on the bag like a kitten focuses on something new, small, and alive that's entered its environment.

The salesman is young, gay, and good. He knows what he's doing. Like a hypnotist, he stops four feet away and gently sways the handbag from side to side. Then he twirls it so I can hone in on the distinctive emblem, the exterior cell phone pocket, the hand-stitching, the gleaming hardware. Instinctively, my hands reach out to the object of my desire.

"Gimme," I say.

"Ah, you like?" he says.

I nod my head. "Gimme."

"You feel compelled to touch it, yes?"

"Like a teenage boy with morning wood."

"Excuse me?"

"Huh?" The spell is broken. I shake my head. "Oh. Sorry. It's an expression."

"An expression?" he says. "Is it popular with beautiful American women?"

"Yes, staggeringly popular," I say, rolling my eyes.

"I'm Georges," he says, producing a business card from thin air. I study the card because I'm curious about the spelling of his name. Because he pronounced it *Zorzay*, if you can just imagine! Georges reminds me of a pretentious waiter friend of mine named Ralph, who calls himself Ricardo. One evening, on a lark, Ralph said, he adopted the foreign name, affected the accent, and doubled his tips.

"Fifteen-fifty," Georges says. Then sighs. "Outrageous, yes?"

"Insane," I say.

"But made for one such as you, I think."

I study the bag without touching it, tell Georges I'll have to think about it. Then I head straight to the jewelry department, while exorcising all thoughts of luxury handbags from my mind.

Until I find myself back in shoes and handbags, minutes after purchasing Sophie's bracelet.

I have to see it one more time.

But I can't find the Gucci.

I look around and see my young, foreign salesman carrying it toward the shoe section, where a stunningly attractive lady in her mid-forties is holding up a pair of Gucci sandals. The two were made for each other, meaning the purse and sandals, and I mean to have them both. It's simple really. All I have to do is change my perspective. If I think of the handbag as an extravagant accessory, I'm toast. Because Georges is absolutely right, it's outrageous. But if I think of the handbag as a mood-enhancer, it could be considered therapy. In other words, it would make me happy.

No, more than that. It would *thrill* me to own this handbag!

I've been years without a shrink. But if I decide to jump back into therapy, only a few sessions would cost more than this handbag. I know people who've been in therapy for many years and are still unhappy. I do the math in my head and realize how lucky I am to have found a handbag that can save me years of therapy.

I start following Georges at a fast clip. Just as I'm about to overtake him, he says to the woman, "If you like to touch teenage boys with morning wood, you will *love* to touch this!"

I abruptly turn and make tracks for the exit.

Chapter 9

SOPHIE'S PUZZLED TO hear I'm changing Tuesday lunch at The Hermitage to Monday dinner at Allez Vous.

"That's too extravagant," she says.

"I struck it rich. Really. You even get a gift!"

"You're overcompensating for something."

"You're my best friend," I say. "You spend tons of money on me. It's the least I can do."

"Lunch is the least you can do. This is something else."

She thinks a minute.

"You're leaving Tuesday," she says.

"Damn, you're good."

"I *am* good. Don't forget it."

"Sorry. About leaving early."

"Hey, it's okay. You've got a life." She pauses, then adds, "A very complicated one."

"Tell me about it!"

"What time are you leaving Tuesday?"

"Early afternoon."

"So we can still do a casual lunch, and save you some money."

"Unacceptable. I've got money burning a hole in my wallet, and I need to spend it on something meaningful. Otherwise I'll end up wasting it on something sensible."

She laughs. "You're a nut."

"See you Monday."

We end the call and I open the door of the closet where I keep my evening wear. I start laying outfits on my bed, trying to decide which one will "speak" to a thirty-five-year-old venture capitalist who's engaged to a wealthy, thirty-year-old woman.

You might think it's just a matter of looking hot, and for most guys, that's probably true. But Joe Fagin's a good-looking guy about to marry serious money. And his fiancé, Carter Teague, is a knockout. He's not going to jeopardize the marriage by having a fling with someone who could come back to haunt him.

Who could come back to haunt him?

A prostitute. A police decoy.

Who else?

Anyone in Carter Teague's social circle or anyone even remotely connected to that world. In other words, I can't play my usual role as the spoiled, party-loving daughter of a wealthy businessman. I have to be—not the opposite of Carter, but I have to *act* differently.

I think about that a minute. A pretty face and a hot body will usually get a man's attention. But what makes a guy like Joe Fagin cheat when he has everything to lose?

Challenge, the thrill of the hunt, and ultimately, the conquest. Followed by no strings and zero chance of future contact.

My plan will have to fit all these elements into a short time frame.

Carter wore an off-the-shoulder leopard tunic, expensive jewelry, and runway sandals. I'll want skinny jeans and a moderately-priced, fashionable top. I'm thinking my long-sleeve navy blouse with black leather trim. It's tasteful enough to get me into Simon Claire's restaurant, should I need to enter, and the jeans are naughty enough to demand Joe Fagin's attention. The blouse is loose-fitting, a nice counterpoint to the tight jeans. Also, it has a boat neckline, which will encourage him to peek down it if I can create the proper angle.

I visualize him sitting at the bar with me.

No. Bar stools are too high. The visual angles are all wrong for bending down to pick up my purse. Of course, I could lean into him, which might give him a quick peek down my top. I'll keep that in mind, but prefer the sight lines that come with him sitting at a table. Of course, I'll need to make sure he's facing the exit. I can bend down to pick up my purse (no, not the Gucci. Even if I'd bought it, which I didn't, the Gucci's too expensive for this job). I'll carry a hundred-dollar faux leather drawstring satchel. When I bend to pick it up, he'll get a quick flash of cleavage. I'll turn and walk away with a natural gait, nothing exotic. It's a biological imperative for men's eyes to be drawn to a woman's backside. If I do my job properly, Joe's eyes will be on my ass like a cheap tattoo.

Chapter 10

AN HOUR LATER I'm in my room at the Brundage, waiting for Carter Teague to call. I'm showered, dressed, ready to go. It's six o'clock.

Fifteen minutes later the phone rings.

"You're cutting it pretty close," I say.

"He checked in late. I wanted to make sure he was in his room before I enter the hotel. It wouldn't do to run into him in the lobby or elevator."

"You're spying on him?"

"No, of course not. I told him to call me when he checked in. What's our room number?"

"You're sixteen-twenty. I'm sixteen-twenty-two."

"Leave my door open so I don't have to knock."

I do, and moments later she enters the room and closes the door behind her.

"I hope I'm doing the right thing," she says.

There's no reason for me to reassure or dissuade her, so I don't respond. She uses the momentary pause to check me out.

"You're not dressed yet?"

"This is what I'm wearing."

"You're joking!"

"You'll have to trust me."

"You look like a college coed!"

"In that case, we're good to go."

She frowns. "Did you use none of the money I gave you to improve your wardrobe?"

I feel my face flush. Carter's wealthy, I'm not. She's six years older, knows her fiancé, and I don't. Still, I know I'm right.

And yet she's managed to intimidate me.

"It almost sounds as though you *want* him to cheat," I say.

"Of *course* not! But I want to see him tested."

"He will be."

"For fifty-five hundred I was hoping to get your A game."

I sigh.

"What, are you going to pout now?" she says.

"When I get back, I'll unlock the connecting door."

"That doesn't make sense. If he enters the room with you, what reason could you possibly give for unlocking the door to the adjoining room?"

"I'll work it out."

"Leave it unlocked," Carter says. "If the door is cracked slightly, and my side is open, I'll hear everything that's going on."

"Leave your door open," I say, "and I'll unlock my side when I get back." By way of explanation, I add, "I'll be gone a couple of hours. I don't want to take a chance someone might plant video equipment in my room."

"Well, I can assure you no one will be allowed to enter your room while you're gone."

I give her a look.

She says, "*What?* You mean *me?* You think I'd do such a thing?"

"I always enter a game trusting the players," I say. "But I'd be a fool not to cut the cards."

"Frankly, I resent your attitude. As well as your choice of wardrobe."

"Just be ready to burst into the room when the clothes come off."

"Burst?"

"I have no intention of standing around in my birthday suit any longer than I have to."

"Shall we use a signal?" she says, mocking me.

"You'll be able to peek through the crack in the door. The minute we're both naked, I'm done."

"You're awfully full of yourself, aren't you?" she says.

"I'll see you later."

I leave her room, enter mine, then lock the connecting door. Then exit my room, close the door behind me, and test to make sure it's locked.

It is.

I retrieve my room key from my purse, and swipe it through the lock. And get a red flash. I swipe it again, slower. Green. It clicks, and I open the door, then close it and retry. This time the door opens after one swipe. I close it and try again. One swipe.

Carter opens the door to her room and peeks at me.

"What are you *doing?*"

"It's a decoy thing," I say. "You wouldn't understand."

"You're a fruitcake, is what you are," she says.

Chapter 11

6:40 P.M.

I take a quick stroll through the bar and restaurant, refreshing the layout in my mind. It's early for the hotel bar crowd, in fact there are only two businessmen in the bar and both of them turn to acknowledge me. One holds his glass up, as if saluting.

I smile, but keep moving.

Simon Claire's is elegant, but I can get in dressed like this. I look around and see only three tables serving guests. But it's early yet. By eight this place will be packed.

I exit the restaurant and stand in the open area between the bar and restaurant, which includes about forty feet of old-world couches and chairs, grouped to encourage pre- and after-dinner conversation. For the time being, I'm alone in this parlor area. Since it's serviced by the bar, it's a perfect place to sit and wait. I can sip a drink while appearing to be deeply involved with my texting. I select a chair that overlooks the elevators, the bar, and the entrance to *Simon Claire's*. To my left there's a small end table and matching chair.

I cross my legs and pretend to send text messages on my cell phone while eyeing the elevator. After a few minutes a waiter appears to take my order.

"Vodka cranberry," I say, without looking up.

He hesitates a moment.

I look up and see Joe Fagin standing over me.

"Oh, I'm so sorry!" I say. "I thought—"

"You thought I was a *waiter?*"

Shit.

"*Seriously?*" he adds.

I laugh. "Can I be honest?"

"Yeah. You can even be *dishonest*, as long as you keep smiling."

I look down, try to force a blush.

I say, "The truth is, I said that without even looking up."

"And now that you see me, I look like what?"

"Honestly? You look like a high-powered businessman."

He bows. "Right answer!" Then he says, "Don't move a muscle. I'll be right back."

He's gone three minutes. When he comes back he's carrying two drinks.

"Vodka cranberry for the lady," he says, "and a bourbon for your lucky date."

He hands me the vodka and sets the bourbon on the table, next to the empty chair.

"What makes you think I've got a date?"

He smiles. "If you don't, you should."

"Well, thanks...I think."

"Do you?"

"Excuse me?"

"Do you have a date?"

"Nope. I'm from Nashville. Just visiting."

"Your grandmother, I hope."

"Huh?" I say, pretending to be confused. Then giggle, and flash a shy smile, as if it took me this long to discern his meaning. It's important for him to think he's smarter than me. He might be, but in case he isn't, I want to hedge my bet. It's also important for me to reel him in, then show him how much fun I am. Reeling him in should be easy, since he's standing over me. I roll my shoulders slightly forward to give him a glimpse of my bra. I'm a 34-C. Not close to Carter's size, but hers are a product of scientific engineering.

Call me paranoid, but I don't trust strange men who bring me drinks. So I say, "I've never tasted bourbon, but I'd like to try it. Here," I say, handing him the vodka. "Taste mine, and I'll taste yours."

His eyes are dancing as he takes a sip, and I expect he's considering making a nasty remark about tasting mine. He decides not to, then a strange expression appears on his face.

"That was damn clever of you," he says.

I look at him with innocent eyes while he adds, "Forcing me to drink what I brought you, in case I slipped something in it.'

I smile. "A girl's got to be careful these days."

"Especially one who looks like you."

I smile, and we touch glasses.

"Cheers," I say.

"Cheers."

We have a sip, and I automatically start tracking the drink count. The first rule of decoy work is you don't allow the mark to get drunk. It's the first excuse they always try. *I was drunk! I didn't know what I was doing!* For this reason, I use the tape recorder app on my cell phone. I record everything that goes down, unless I'm using the phone for one of the games I play to keep the mark interested.

"Mind if I sit down?" he says.

"If you're waiting for your *wife*, I do!"

He holds up his bare ring finger.

"That's your proof?" I say, giggling.

"I'd tell you to check my pockets to see if there's a ring in there, but I don't think you're that kind of girl. You're not, right?"

I look down again and smile, unsure how to answer that. I've learned when it comes to picking up men who cheat, when in doubt, remain silent and smile. Men like shy, mysterious women. It worked for Jackie Kennedy, it'll work for me.

"I hope I didn't offend you," he says.

"I'm single too," I say, holding up my bare ring finger.

"That's your proof?" he says, laughing.

I give him my bubbly laugh. Since he's still standing over me, I roll my shoulders forward again, offering him another quick peek.

He thinks I'm fun. That's a good thing, because in my wildest dreams I can't imagine Carter Teague being fun or playful. In my experience, guys seeking a fling want something different. If their wives are stuffy, they'll settle for stuffy, but what they want is playful. If their wives are B cups, they'll settle for B's, but what really revs them up is an A or C cup. If their wives are heavy, they'll settle for heavy, but they'll work harder to bed someone thin. If their wives are domineering, they want demure. If sweet, they want bitchy. And if their significant other has fake boobs, they'll be craving the real thing.

I look up at him suddenly, and catch him looking down my blouse. We both look away, embarrassed. Then we look back at each other and pretend it never happened.

"Were you planning to have dinner here at the hotel?" he says.

I glance at the entrance to Simon Claire's.

"Too expensive," I say.

"And yet you were sitting here."

"I was actually searching for nearby restaurants on my cell phone."

"Find any?"

"A few. But I was still trying to decide."

"Would you consider having dinner with me? It'll be my treat."

"Where?"

"Here."

"Are you alone?"

"I had plans, but I'm willing to cancel them."

I pretend I'm thinking about it. "I don't even know your name."

"Jim," he lies. "Jim Davenport." He extends his hand, and we shake.

"I'm Marcie Lane."

"Marcie, I can honestly say you're the most beautiful woman I've ever seen in person."

I leave his compliment hanging in the air to show I'm not impressed by flattery. I purse my lips and say, "I'm probably dressed too casual for this place."

"Nonsense!" he says. "Your outfit's perfect!"

"Are you sure?"

"Come," he says. "It's just dinner, and we're both stranded in Louisville."

I pause a moment, catch his eye, and say, "Well, why not?"

Chapter 12

THE MAITRE D' SEATS us, and Joe orders the same drinks he brought me a few minutes ago.

"What brings you to Louisville?" Joe asks.

"My job interview ran late, so the company offered to put me up at the hotel. I could've driven back, but it sounded like an adventure."

"Because?"

I laugh. "I don't normally get to stay in such a fancy place."

"They're probably going to hire you."

"You think?"

"Otherwise, they wouldn't have offered the room. What type of job is it?"

"I'm an illustrator for children's books."

He pretends to be amazed, and says he has "zero artistic skills." I expect him to ask me to draw him a picture while we're waiting to order, and I'm artistic enough to do it. But he doesn't. Instead, he asks to be excused.

I know what he's doing. Cancelling his dinner plans. I see him taking out his cell phone while walking out the front door. I take this opportunity to make my signature move. I whip out my lipstick and write the words, *Call Me!* on a napkin, along with my phone number. I remove another napkin from my purse, one I'd prepared earlier, and place it under the table.

Then I sneak into the kitchen, and tell one of the waiters I'm playing a trick on my boyfriend, and get him to escort me to the service elevator. He does, and I take it to the third floor. Then I backtrack down the hall till I'm looking down onto the parlor, where Joe's finishing his call. He looks from side to side, then goes back in the restaurant. When he does, I go to the elevator and press the button. When it arrives, I climb on and wait.

I've done this a dozen times, so I know exactly what's happening. As Joe makes his way back to the table, he'll see I'm not there. He'll assume I've gone to the ladies' room. He might look around to see where it's located, might even decide to stand outside the ladies' room to escort me back to the table. But Simon Claire's doesn't have restrooms inside the restaurant, so Joe will reclaim his seat at the table, at which point he'll notice the lipstick note on the napkin. At first he'll be pissed, thinking I've ditched him. He'll assume the phone number's a fake, and won't want to call. But he'll call. And when he does...

My phone rings.

It's Joe.

"Hi handsome!" I say, with great enthusiasm.

"Is everything okay?" I can hear the relief in his voice. He's unsure what's happening, but likes the fact I gave him my real number. And he's got to feel good that I called him handsome.

"I'm hiding," I say. "Come find me."

"You're...what?"

"Hiding."

"Where?"

"If I tell you where, it won't be fun."

I know what he's doing. Looking around, trying to see if I'm sitting at another table with a menu covering my face.

He says, "Give me a hint."

I say, "Look under the table."

"You're not under the table," he says.

"Look anyway," I say.

At this point he's looking around to see if I'm watching him. He's slightly put out. On the other hand, I'm still on the phone and haven't ditched him. He's not thrilled I'm making him jump through hoops, and doesn't like being made to feel stupid or out of control. But he has to admit, I'm certainly different than Carter Teague. By now he's found the second napkin, the one where I wrote, "take the left lobby elevator to the third floor."

"Is your room on the third floor?" he says.

"No."

"Oh."

I hang up. While I'm waiting, someone has pressed the button, and I ride to the tenth floor. A man gets on and rides with me to the lobby. He waits for me to exit, but I say, "Thanks anyway, but I'm going back up for a minute."

He looks at me strangely, but leaves.

I press the button for the third floor. When I get there the doors open, then close. Then the elevator starts moving down...

Chapter 13

WHEN THE ELEVATOR doors open, Joe's standing there with a surprised look on his face.

"You found me!" I squeal, and plant a quick kiss on his mouth. He's so stunned he doesn't have time to react. He looks from side to side, making sure no one's watching, then moves in for another kiss. But I put my finger between our lips and whisper, "Dessert comes *after* dinner!"

I slide past him and start heading back to the restaurant. Then stop and turn and wait for him to join me. He's practically glaring at me, but takes his cue and walks toward me slowly, trying to appear cool. As we walk through the parlor, he startles me by grabbing my ass. It takes me by surprise and seriously annoys me, since it wasn't just a pat. He actually placed his hand on my butt and slid it down and cupped the bottom of my cheeks. I have to bite my lip to keep from making a scene. I know I'm walking a fine line here, enticing men to cheat while expecting them to be gentlemen. I also know there's another word for decoy work.

Prick teaser.

Much as I hate to admit it, I'm purposely getting these men all hot and bothered, knowing in the end their lives might be destroyed. While I can make a case their lives *should* be destroyed if they're cheating on their loved ones, there are times, especially when children are involved in a marriage, I worry if I'm doing the right thing. I mean, I know it's not the right thing. What I ask myself, *is it a necessary thing?*

As we get back to the table I'm really steamed. I tell myself, *Let it go, Dani. Keep your eyes on the prize.* But I nearly come unglued when he asks, "Did you like that back there, what I did?"

"Excuse me?"

"Did that feel good?"

I dig my fingernails into the sides of the chair and force a smile.

There's a reason I play the *Call Me!* game. Actually, several reasons. First, it shows I'm fun and playful, something men usually seek in a younger woman. It reminds them of when their wives were fun and playful. Second, it gives them a chance to hunt for me, which usually has a better effect than it did on Joe. Men like the thrill of the hunt, the chase, and capturing their prey. My little game allows them to do all three. At the end, they receive a kiss. Not saying a kiss from me is the highlight of their lives, but it's fun, and lets them know I'm "into them."

The game I play usually involves letting them peek down my blouse a few times. If I'm wearing a dress they might get a flash of leg or panties. If there's a limo involved, I always wear a short skirt. What I'm saying, I know I'm playing with fire. I'm well aware it's hypocritical of me to get annoyed when a man touches me inappropriately. On the other hand, income tax auditors are paid to catch cheaters, and no one ever tries to grope them!

There are typically three places I have to be prepared to fend off amorous advances. The first is in the elevator, when we're going up to my room. If we're alone in the elevator, most guys will use that as an opportunity to cop a feel or steal a kiss.

My solution? Enter the elevator with others present. Barring that, I'll say there's a camera in the elevator, so he needs to be a good boy till we get to the room. The cheaters always keep their heads down and look the other way.

The second time I'm vulnerable is when we're walking down the hall toward my room. For some reason, guys think this is a good place to try to pat my behind, or stand me against a wall like they do in the movies, where the hero gives the girl a long, sensual, tongue kiss. On the big screen, this move always reduces the love interest to putty and leaves her panting for more. My solution for avoiding this? When the elevator doors open to my floor I push the mark backward, off balance, and yell, "Tag! You're it!" Then I run full speed to my room, giggling all the way.

The final place I'm most apt to be mauled is when we're standing at the door to my hotel room, and I'm trying to make the key card work. This is the place they always want to reach their arms around me and cup my breasts. My only solution is to have the key in my hand when I exit the elevator. Unfortunately, hotel key cards are unreliable, and by the time I get to my room door, he's caught me.

In most cases the seduction has gone on for well over an hour before we get to the "Tag, you're it!" phase. By the time we arrive at the door to my room most of these guys are worked up to the point they're willing to face a rape charge. So the longer it takes to get inside the door, the more places on my body they're able to grope.

For this reason, I always practice getting the key card to work before meeting the mark.

Simon Claire's dinner service is painfully slow. I order a spinach salad and grilled chicken. Joe's a steak and potatoes guy. He'd normally order the chopped salad, he says, but doesn't want me to smell onions on his breath later on.

What a guy!

Speaking of guys, some are all confidence, others need constant reassurance. Joe's a member of the second camp. He's touching me every chance he gets, as if my allowing it gets us one step closer to sex.

It's driving me batty! Especially the part where he looks around the room just before touching me, to make sure no one he knows has entered the room. He does it every single time! Could he possibly be a more obvious cheater? If I knew nothing about the guy I'd know he was cheating.

If I reach for my drink he puts his hand on mine and looks to see if I'm smiling.

I am.

When he tells me how wealthy and clever he is, he punctuates each point by patting my arm or, when he can get to it, my thigh. He's staring at me in such a creepy and lustful way I loathe myself for putting up with it.

He's had a couple of drinks.

I can tell he's in complete control of his faculties, but he's pretending to slur his words slightly, using the liquor as an excuse to speak more suggestively. As dinner drags on, he's becoming more aggressive, as well.

The low point comes when he insists we check out the dessert menu. He scoots his chair toward me till his right arm brushes my left. As he holds the menu in front of us with his left hand, he reaches up and grabs my boob with his right. I expect him to remove it as fast as he put it there, but he doesn't. He's rubbing and cupping my breast, and rubbing his thumb where he thinks my nipple is.

He's doing all this while studying my face and pretending to tell me what's on the menu in the cheesiest possible way. I show him the best smile I can force, and allow him to continue feeling me up. He's getting ninety percent padded bra, but the ten percent that's me wants to slit his throat. Finally, mercifully, the waiter approaches, and Joe Asshole removes his hand and announces, "We've decided to skip dessert."

He hands the waiter a credit card and says, "Can you prepare the check?"

The waiter thanks Joe and leaves to fetch the bill. I wonder if he'll bring it back and say something like, "It's been a pleasure, Mr. Fagin!"

If he does, I wonder how Joe (Jim Davenport) Fagin will respond. I can't believe the guy is dumb enough to use a fake name and pay with a credit card! One part of me thinks he can't be this green. But the part of me that's been fondled and probed the past two hours disagrees vehemently.

This guy's a first-class puke.

Joe says, "How was dinner?"

Though I've complimented the dinner several times tonight, he wants to remind me he's shelled out some cash. Once again I reply, "Incredible!" But this time I add, "Did you enjoy your steak?"

"Frankly, I've had better. But not better company."

We remain silent a full minute while he stares at me with lust in his heart. Then he says, "Do you even have a clue how hot you are?"

"Tell me."

"If I poured a pitcher of ice water on your crotch, the steam coming off it would form a rain cloud."

"You think?"

"I do. In fact, I'm gonna call you Princess Rain Cloud."

I want to retch, but say, "You're so sweet!"

He's not sweet, he's a cartoon. But I force myself to remember every word so Sophie and I can have a big laugh about it on Monday.

While we wait for the check, Joe looks around the room before saying, "I'll pay the bill and you'll come to my room for champagne. Maybe we'll order some chocolate-covered strawberries. Unless you'd rather have ice cream?"

"I've had the best time," I say, "but I'm getting a little tired, and I've got a long drive ahead of me tomorrow. Maybe we should call it a night."

He looks at me as if I'd slapped his face.

I wish I had.

But I hear myself say, "On the other hand, you've been so sweet, I hate to say goodnight. Would you like to come to my room and raid the mini bar?"

"I'd *love* to!"

The check comes, and we head for the elevator.

Chapter 14

THE PARLOR AREA is busy, and there are two elderly couples waiting by the elevator. When the doors open, we follow them on. According to the lit buttons, we'll be the first ones off. With a guy as "handsy" as Joe, I definitely want to sprint to my room, but I can't very well push him backwards to get a head start, since I might injure one of the old people. As the elevator doors close, I remove my stilettos and place them in my bag. Then I remove my room key and hold it in my right hand.

As we exit, I shout, "Sixteen-twenty-two!" and start running full speed toward my room, while giggling. Joe's not the type to run down the hall giggling, but he does follow me at a respectable rate of speed. Thankfully the door opens on the first swipe, and I turn the deadbolt so the door won't lock when I close it behind me. Knowing I have ten seconds at most, I race to the back of the room, unlock the door to the adjoining room and crack it a quarter inch. I start walking back toward the front door as Joe enters.

"How do you want to do this?" he says, in a low voice.

"What do you mean?"

"I mean, how do you like it? Gentle or rough?"

I'm glad my phone's recording all this. He'll have a hard time explaining himself to Carter later on, assuming she can't hear him.

"I'd prefer we turn the lights off," I say.

"I'd prefer we leave them on."

"Let's compromise. We'll leave one light on."

"Two."

"Okay, but I get to choose."

"Whatever."

I choose the desk lamp behind me and the entry way light, and turn off all the others.

"I can barely see you!" he complains, then turns on one of the nightstand lamps. He clicks it two more times, to the highest setting, then walks to the end of the bed and sits. Now I'm standing a mere four feet in front of him. I take two steps back. The lamplight is completely illuminating me, and it's obviously his intention to take full advantage of the view.

I sigh, and tell myself to just deal with it, now that we're in the home stretch.

"Take off your top," he says.

"You first."

He takes off his shirt, then says, "Now you."

I lift my blouse over my head and carefully lay it over the back of the desk chair.

"You're so precise," he says. "Now the jeans."

"You're still wearing shoes. I'm not."

He takes off his shoes and socks. Then says, "Lose the pants."

"You first," I say, but he says, "It's your turn to go first."

I shrug, lower my jeans to my ankles, and step out of them. Then drape the jeans over the blouse.

"Your turn," I say.

"I'm down to jeans," he says. "You're still wearing bra and panties."

"So?"

"It's two to one. I'm not wearing any underwear."

"Prove it."

"I'll prove it after you take off the bra."

I can't believe we're having this conversation. I remove my bra and place it over the rest of my clothes on the chair.

"Nice tits," he says, his voice suddenly husky. "Those are *real* nice."

"Your turn," I say.

He stands and steps out of his pants.

"You lied," I say, pointing at his underwear.

"Sue me," he says.

He points at my panties and says, "Show me what's doing under there."

"You first."

He takes a menacing step toward me, then thinks better of it. I hope he doesn't notice how close I am to being terrified. While I know Carter's about to burst into the room, this guy is so creepy I can't help but wonder *what if?*

What if she fell asleep? What if she left the room and locked herself out? What if...

He steps out of his underwear. I won't go into details.

"Now you," he says.

I take a couple more steps back and wriggle out of my panties.

"You're not shaved," he says.

I turn to look for Carter.

Joe says, "I'd have taken you for shaved."

I take another step back, toward the door that leads to Carter's room.

Joe says, "I've gotta say, I'm surprised to see you're a natural blonde. I'd have bet money you weren't. But your bush is darker than your hair, so I'm not *completely* wrong. What do *you* think, Carter?"

I spin around to see Carter Teague standing in the doorway in her bra and panties, taking my picture with her cell phone. I jump behind the chair.

"I'd say she's a honey blonde," Carter says. Then adds, "Happy birthday, darling."

I turn to Joe. He's grinning.

"Thank you, darling," he says. "She's everything you promised. And more!"

I look at Carter. "You set me up!"

She smiles.

I say, "You're *okay* with this?

She shrugs and says, "Joe likes the pretty girls. I like Joe. It's his birthday."

I grab my panties and start putting them on.

"I'll give you an extra two grand to fuck him," she says.

Normally I'd jump to my feet and slap her, but I don't want to deal with Joe. This is a scene that could turn ugly in a hurry. I fumble around with my bra. My hands are shaking, and it's not happening.

"Three grand," Joe says, "if you'll do both of us."

"*I'm not a whore!*" I shout.

"Maybe, maybe not," he says. "But you're certainly a stripper."

I'm shaking with fury, trembling with fear. And can't get the freaking bra to work. It dawns on me to give up on the bra. I scramble into my jeans, toss my blouse on, and stuff the bra in my handbag. I pause, because there's something else in the room I don't want to leave behind.

But Joe's standing between me and the thing I need.

The three of us are at angles to each other, and something happened while I was getting dressed. Something I feel, but can't explain. Something about the vibe in the room.

It's suddenly taken a dangerous shift.

Joe's staring at me and stroking himself, and I don't like the look in his eyes. I decide to make a run for the door.

Before I take the first step, Carter says, "You know what we can do?"

"What's that?" Joe says.

"We can rape her."

Chapter 15

"WE CAN RAPE her," Carter repeats, "and there's nothing she can do about it."

"Because you paid her five grand for sex," Joe says.

"Plus expenses."

Carter locks the connecting door. Joe dashes to the main door, locks it, and sets the metal latch. While he's busy doing that, I run to the bed and grab the thing I didn't want to leave behind.

My Glock 26.

I pull it from under the mattress and point it at Carter.

"*Jesus!*" she says. "I was just *kidding!*"

"I don't think so," I say.

"You wouldn't *dare* shoot me," she says.

I pull the slide back and release it, and now all three of us know the angry blonde with the shaky hands is holding a gun with a live round in the chamber. Since I'm pointing it at Carter's face, I'm not surprised to see her assume a defensive posture, with her head turned away, hands in front of her face. I'm a little surprised to see the torrent of pee leaking through her panties, dribbling down her legs, though I'd probably pee my pants too, if I were in her situation.

"Drop your phone on the floor and kick it to me," I say.

She does.

"Now sit down."

She looks around. "Where?"

"On the floor."

She sits in her pee.

I turn the gun on Joe and notice his erection has collapsed.

"Nothing says shrinkage like a loaded Glock," I say. "Go sit on the floor by your girlfriend."

"She's my wife, actually," Joe says. "And we really *were* kidding about raping you."

When he's on the floor beside her I rush to the door, unlock it, and remove the latch. As I do that, I hear Carter say, "I am so *fucking* turned on!"

I open the door, step into the hall, and hear Joe say, "This is the best birthday present I ever had!"

I put the gun in my handbag, close the door, and head for the elevator.

Chapter 16

MONDAY EVENING

"WERE THEY SERIOUS, do you think?"

"About raping me?"

Sophie nods.

"At the time, yes, absolutely."

"But now that you've had a few days to think about it?"

"Now I'm not so sure."

"Because of what they said when you were leaving the room?"

I nod. "I think they might have been acting out a part. Like some sort of twisted foreplay."

"Did you keep her cell phone?"

"I put it under my tire and ran over it a couple of times. Then picked up the pieces and tossed them out the window along I-71."

Sophie laughs, and pours some Sauterne in her wine glass. Then tops off mine.

"This has been the most wonderful birthday dinner ever!" she says.

We touch glasses.

She adds, "I can only think of two things that would make it better."

"Here it comes," I say.

She smiles. "Dare I ask how it went with Ben?"

I sigh. "Vicky was a bust."

"Vicky being?"

"Vicky Stringfellow. The schoolteacher."

"Ah. You met her."

"I did."

We take another sip of our dessert wine.

Sophie says, "Let me guess. You told her he's married."

"Yes."

"To you."

"Yes."

She shakes her head. "I can think of at least ten ways to get a woman interested in Ben. Surprisingly, none of them involve disclosing your marital status."

"Go figure," I say.

"Have you in fact spoken to Ben yet?"

"No. But here's the thing—"

She waves my words away with her hand. "If any part of your explanation involves the analogy about the lemon in the vodka bottle, I might emit a loud scream."

"Orange."

"Excuse me?"

"It's an orange, not a lemon. In the vodka bottle."

"Whatever."

"If you think about it, it's a beautiful sentiment. He's the bottle, I'm the orange. The only way I can get out is by crushing me or shattering him."

"There's another way to look at it," she says.

I wait.

"You're the orange, right? And he's the bottle?"

I nod.

"He's holding you prisoner."

I raise my eyebrows. Sophie might be onto something. I think about it while she pours the last bit of Sauterne in my glass. Then I say, "I'm meeting a woman from my yoga class."

"About Ben?"

"Yup."

"When?"

"Thursday morning after class."

"Are you going to screw it up?"

"Probably."

She shakes her head. "Can I make an observation?"

"No."

She laughs. "It's my birthday, I get to make an observation."

"Go ahead. Pretend you're my mom."

"The deal with the women? It's not working."

"That's your observation?"

"No. My observation is it's not going to work."

"You're probably right."

"You need to tell him, Dani."

I nod.

"You won't be happy till you do."

"I know."

"Say you'll do it."

"I'll do it."

"Do you mean it this time?"

I nod. Because it's easier to nod than to ask your loving husband for a divorce.

Sophie starts to say something, changes her mind.

"What?"

"Nothing. I'm the slightest bit tipsy."

"No secrets, Sofe. That's the cornerstone of our friendship."

She winces. "I was just going to say, if you ever find yourself in that type of situation where someone might be after you..."

I'm trying to follow. "You mean like Joe Fagin?"

"Yes."

"What about him?"

"If you think he's going to be a problem..."

I give her an amused look. "What, you'll set him straight for me?"

I laugh.

She laughs.

Then says, "Not me. My uncle."

"What uncle?"

"Uncle Sal."

"Sounds like a quiet, older guy who wears a sweater and runs a deli."

She laughs. "Forget it."

We're both glowing from the buzz. I say, "Your best friend is in trouble, but don't worry?"

"Yeah, that's right," she says, "Because I know a guy who knows a guy!"

"Uncle Sal from the deli?"

"Exactly."

"Gee, I wish I'd known that, Sofe. I could've scared the shit out of Joe and Carter. 'You threatening me? I'm connected. Ever hear the name Uncle Sal?' And Joe's face would go white, and he'd say, 'The deli guy? Oh, shit, Ms. Ripper, not the deli guy!' But it's too late because Sal has already called in sick. By sundown he'll force them to eat an unusually tough cut of pastrami."

She chuckles. "You're too much."

I laugh, and say, "So who's uncle Sal? Really?"

She looks around, then lowers her voice, and whispers, "Sal Bonadello."

"*What?* The *mob boss?*"

"*Shhh!* Jesus, Dani, lower your voice, will you?"

I lower my voice. "You're *joking*, right?"

"He's my uncle."

I frown at her. "How long have we been best friends? A year?"

"More than a year."

This time I look around before lowering my voice. "You're related to a *mob boss*? How could you not *tell* me that?"

"It's not the sort of information that encourages close friendships."

"How close are you?"

"Me and Sal?"

I nod.

"He's my father's brother."

"Um...your parents are deceased, right? Like mine?"

"In Italian families, it's as if no one ever dies. Sal and Marie wanted to take me in. He wanted to take an interest in my career. So I moved here."

I push my nose to one side, like a gangster, and try to sound like one. "My niece, Sophie. Got a voice like a songbird. You oughta hire her. Be a shame if your club burned down."

"Exactly."

"Last time I checked, Alexander's not an Italian name."

"It's my stage name. My real one's Sophie Bonadello."

I shake my head. "Mafia princess?"

She shrugs.

"You could have me whacked?"

She frowns. "See? This is why I don't tell you things. Forget I ever brought it up."

"You mean Fuhgeddaboudit?"

She shakes her head, laughing. "You," she says.

"What?"

"You're something else, you are."

Chapter 17

I'VE GOT A bedroom at Sophie's house. This is where I come on Mondays and Tuesdays to get away. It's how I stay sane. I've got clothes in the closet, personal items in the bathroom, got my own sheets and pillows on the bed.

Sophie's a singer-songwriter, living in Nashville. But she's not really a singer. I mean, she's got a fine, melodic voice, and she sings around town when she can. It's just that she can't support herself singing.

Songwriting's a different story.

Sophie's famous. You might not know her name, but you know her songs. She's written hits for all the young country stars, and a couple of pop stars as well. She's won three Grammys, same as Elvis.

But unlike Elvis, Sophie's in love with me.

We're not lovers.

Sophie's made it clear she's interested. You know, in a relationship. A sexual relationship.

I've never done that. You know, with a woman.

But I want to.

It's just that...I'm married.

Sophie's my best friend and confidante. And though she loves me and clearly aches for us to be together, she would never rush me, never push me, never want me to do anything I wasn't ready to do. So we live together two days a week, and we've fashioned a celibate mini-life together, within the framework of our real lives.

She's twenty-nine, I'm twenty-four. Except for Ben, Sophie's the only person on earth who knows what happened to me nine years ago. I'm incredibly fortunate these two wonderful, caring people have found me.

But Ben found me first.

I pay the bill despite Sophie's insistence on taking care of the wine.

"I still don't feel right about you spending all this money," she says.

"Deal with it."

I hand her a birthday card with a long, girly note about what she's meant to me this year. She reads it and starts crying. Watching her cry makes me cry. We see each other crying and that makes us both laugh. Then I hand her the gift. She opens it, sees the bracelet, and starts crying again.

"I'll treasure this," she says, putting it on.

I smile, knowing it's true.

In a very quiet voice she says, "I love you, Dani. You have no idea how much."

"I love you too, Sofe," I say, using her nickname.

That night we do what we always do before going to bed. Put on the most outrageous pajama tops and bottoms we can find, and hang out in her den and talk and laugh for hours.

My house in Cincinnati has one upstairs bedroom, Sophie's house in Nashville has two. Both have master bedrooms on the first floor. But on Mondays and Tuesdays, Sophie sleeps in the vacant upstairs bedroom to be closer to me.

I love that about her.

When we're all talked out we walk up the stairs together like we always do, and hug each other goodnight. Over the months we've been together the hugs have gotten longer and more intimate, though nothing sexual has taken place.

Yet.

But during these moments when we're in each other's arms, and our bodies are touching, and I close my eyes and feel her heartbeat, I get flushed, off-balance, and almost completely out of control.

Almost.

Could I ever be truly satisfied and fulfilled being in a long-term relationship with a woman?

I honestly don't know.

Could Sophie?

She doesn't know either, but she thinks so.

"You're too pretty to be with a man," she once said. "We need you on our team."

"*Your* team?" I laughed. "You're barely on the team yourself!"

So yes, we've talked about it, but the bottom line is we're both newbies. Sophie's had seven sexual experiences in her life and only two of them were women.

"Every night we hug vertically," she says. "Just once I'd like us to hug horizontally."

I laugh. "You always say that."

"And yet you never take me up on it."

"I don't trust myself."

She pulls back and grins. "You've never said *that* before!"

"Guess you're wearing me down."

"My evil plan is working?"

"Seems to be."

She pretends to do a little cheer. Then says, "Yay!"

She kisses my cheek.

I kiss hers and say, "Happy birthday, Sofe."

"At the risk of sounding like Joe Fagin," she says, "This is the best birthday ever!"

We laugh.

"I'll leave my door open tonight," she says. "In case you change your mind."

I laugh. "You always say that, too."

Chapter 18

TUESDAY EVENING

BEN AND I are standing in the bar at Johnny Prime, Cincinnati's legendary steakhouse, awaiting the entrance of his overachieving college roommate, Roy Burroughs. Ben has warned me Roy is not only charming, but a force of nature, and I need to realize he's a complete and total player.

"He's going to be all over you," he warns.

"I'd find that terribly rude."

"Doesn't matter. He thinks he's God's gift to women. Thinks he can get anyone he wants."

"What are you saying?"

Ben laughs. "He's brutally handsome. Or was, at least. In any case, I'm counting on you not to fall in love with him."

"Fat chance."

"Good. Because that would sort of destroy the whole concept of me having something the great Roy Burroughs could never get."

"Tell me again about that."

"When Roy sees us together his face is going to drop! The last thought in his head when he leaves tonight will be me holding you. It'll be like I'm the one standing in the end zone instead of him, spiking the ball after scoring the winning touchdown. He'll see you, and I won't have to say a word. He'll know I finally beat him at something. Seriously, Dani, I can't thank you enough."

I give him a look.

"What?" he says.

"I hope you can come up with a better way to express the sentiment. Because right now you're making me feel like a dirty old football."

Ben winks. "Coming from a guy, that's a hell of a compliment. Except for the old part."

"And the dirty part."

He winks again. "That's up for debate."

Ben's in the best mood tonight! I hope it goes the way he wants, but honestly, how could it? I mean, he's got such high expectations. Do things ever turn out great when you're trying to show someone else up?

"Ben?"

"Yes?"

"I know you think I'm beautiful," I say, "But what if Roy shows up with someone who's *truly* gorgeous? Someone who makes me look like dog meat?"

"First of all, there's no such woman, because you're spectacular. Second, it's not just your looks, it's the whole package. Your personality, your charm, your intelligence. You're sweet, kind, and classy. What I'm saying, looks can be bought. The rest is you. I've given up sex, warmth, and intimacy...and two nights every week just to be able to live with you!"

"Thanks."

"*Thanks?*"

"I know you meant that as a compliment, but the last part came across a little bitter. Not that I don't deserve it."

He thinks about what he said. "I get that. I'm sorry."

"You have every right to feel that way. I just hate that I've done this to you."

"Done what?" a voice says from behind us.

We turn, and it's not Roy Burroughs's jaw that drops.

It's mine.

Chapter 19

ROY BURROUGHS IS in a wheelchair.

And he's not nearly as good-looking as Ben led me to believe.

Of course, it's been a long time since Ben's seen Roy. What's it been, sixteen years? Something like that. A lot can happen to a person's looks in sixteen years. You hear it all the time from those who go to high school class reunions. Some look the same, but most don't.

But that's not what makes my jaw drop when I meet Roy Burroughs.

What makes my jaw drop is I know Roy's a fake. He's pretending to be confined to a wheelchair. I know this as certainly as I know my real name is Mindy Renee Whittaker.

That's right, my current name, Dani Ripper, is as fake as Roy's wheelchair.

People use phony names for different reasons. Some do it to deceive people. Others, like me, change their names to create a new life. Wait, maybe these are the same reasons, since they both involve deception.

I won't argue the point.

But I didn't change my name in order to hurt people, or take advantage of them. I did it to protect myself. I went to court to change my name because I got sick of being stalked by the media. Sick of seeing my filthy, bruised and bloody fifteen-year-old face on TV every time the next young, pretty girl got abducted. Sick of being Mindy Renee Whittaker, "the little girl who got away." Sick of being the poster child for the precious few who manage to escape their captors. Sick of being contacted by grief-stricken parents clinging to their last ounce of hope.

I couldn't give them hope, because I didn't think any other fifteen-year-old girls would do what I was willing to do in order to escape.

I know Roy's faking the wheelchair because I've actually met him once before. On that occasion he had full use of his legs. That was four days ago, and he was going by the name Joe Fagin. As he and I look at each other now, only one of us is shocked.

Me.

When he gives me a shit-eating grin it becomes crystal clear what really happened last week with Carter Teague. I don't know if she and Roy are married or engaged, or if she's some hooker or decoy Roy hired to play the part. What I *do* know is Roy Burroughs found a way to beat my husband yet again.

Because Roy Burroughs has seen Ben's wife completely naked. Not only that, he kissed me, groped me, and felt me up. And now he gets to play a game that ridicules my sweet, innocent husband. Roy's going to allow Ben to believe he's finally won.

If I'm lucky.

If I'm not lucky, Roy's going to play Ben for a fool all through dinner, and humiliate him with the truth for dessert.

Chapter 20

BEN'S FACE IS white. He can't get over the fact Roy's in a wheelchair. I see him struggling with what to say about it, how to approach the subject. Roy's grinning at me, sharing the joke. I glare at him until Ben looks at me, at which point I become all smiles.

"Ben, you're right!" Roy says. "She's absolutely stunning!"

Ben looks at me and beams. "She is, isn't she."

"I'd give a week's pay to see her naked," Roy adds, and winks at me.

"Well, that's not going to happen," I say.

Ben moves closer to me, as if to protect me.

Roy says, "Trust me, I know Ben's feelings about that! He's been raving about you for years! I finally had to come to town and see for myself what all the fuss was about. And now that I've seen you in the flesh, I feel I've known you forever. Can I call you Honey?"

A reference to my bush.

"I told you Roy was a charmer," Ben says.

"You did," I say. Addressing Roy, I add, "Given your history as a charmer, I'd feel more comfortable if you called me Dani, as in Ben's wife, Dani."

Ben looks mildly uncomfortable. "Well, I didn't mean to imply..."

Roy interrupts, "No, of course not! No harm done." He smiles. "Dani's clearly onto me! Yes, I may be a charmer, but I know true love when I see it."

Ben's face goes from concerned to all smiles. A waitress brings Roy a shot of bourbon, neat. "Keep 'em comin', Monica," Roy says, "maybe I'll give you a car for a tip."

"If you do, I'll give you a ride!" she giggles.

Roy looks at me and winks. "What do you suppose Monica means by that?"

We look at her and she giggles again. "Oh dear," she says.

"Catch me again when we get a table," he says.

"Will do!" Monica says cheerfully, then flits off to find another flirt.

"They must know you here," I say.

"Nah. I ordered the drink when I came in. Gave her a fifty." He looks at me and says, "Women will do anything for cash."

"Some women," Ben says.

Roy gives him a smug look. "Well said, Benny Boy."

He downs it in a single motion, and Ben and I exchange a look.

The hostess finds us in the bar and escorts us to our table. A busboy removes a chair so Roy can park his wheelchair in its place. Our waiter introduces himself and sees we have our drinks, so he tells us the specials and hands us menus. We study them a few minutes. When he comes back, we place our orders.

"What type of work do you do, Roy?" I ask.

"I'm an investor. Businesses, Real estate, horses, you name it. If there's money in it, I'll find it!" Then he says, "What about you, Dani? What do *you* do?"

"I'm a housewife."

Roy laughs. "I know better than that! Our Ben has kept me informed through the years. It must be terribly exciting to be a private investigator."

"The truth is I get very little work. Most of the time I'm a housewife, and quite content to be one, though I wasn't aware you and Ben spoke on such a regular basis."

"I check in with him once or twice a year, though now that I think about it, he never calls me. What's with *that*, Benny Boy?"

Ben says, "I figure you're so busy all the time! I'm always afraid I'll interrupt some high-level business meeting. You're always in motion. I was just telling Dani, you're a force of nature!"

Roy says, "Well, thanks, but *you've* managed to do something I've never accomplished."

"I can't imagine what that might be," Ben says. "You're wealthy, successful, brilliant...you've had a wonderful life."

"I can't complain, and thanks for calling me brilliant. But with all my success, I've never found true love, and that's the greatest success of all. I'm truly happy for you!"

"Thank you," Ben says. "That means a lot to me."

As Roy looks at me his eyes tear up. I wonder how he does that. Does he keep a cut onion in his pocket and rub his eyes with onion juice when I'm not looking?

He says, "I'm happy for you, too, Dani. Because Ben's not only my best friend, he's also the best human being I've ever met. Of course, I don't have to tell *you* how special he is!"

"True," I say, "But it's always nice to hear my husband complimented."

"I'd never do *anything* to hurt him," Roy adds, holding my gaze.

"I'm sure you wouldn't. I mean, what type of friend *would?*"

Ben says, "Thanks, Roy. You've always been a good friend."

Monica brings Roy another drink and asks if we'd like something.

"I think we're good," Ben says. He and I are still nursing the drinks we ordered before Roy showed up.

"Benny never could hold his liquor," Roy says. "I could tell you stories, but I wouldn't want to embarrass my best friend. Not in front of his wife, anyway."

Ben shows a smile, but it's a sad one.

I know what's going on in Ben's mind. He's feeling guilty for all the negative remarks he made about Roy. Now he sees Roy's looks have faded a bit, sees him in a

96

wheelchair, sees him drinking too much. Of course, Roy's enjoying every moment of Ben's discomfort, narcissistic bully that he is. And what makes him truly evil is he's pulled me into his ugly game so I can watch him dismantle my husband's ego.

What a complete bully he is! I can't imagine what sort of high he could possibly get by emasculating my husband in front of me. According to Ben it's been going on since the day they met.

Dinner arrives and we dig in. The men talk to each other about their college days, and I try to remember everything Carter Teague said and did last week, and everything Roy, as Joe Fagin, said and did.

The one thing I keep coming back to is Joe's final comment: *"This is the best birthday present I ever had!"*

At the time I thought he meant I was the first part of the present, like an appetizer to whet his appetite, and having sex with his "wife," Carter, was the rest of the present. I know some couples watch porn together before having sex, and I figured Carter and Joe had taken this concept to the next level. Perhaps they intended to take it up another notch as well, since they offered me three grand to have sex with them. I wouldn't have done that for any amount of money, but what if I had? Poor Ben would be even more devastated.

Now I realize Roy's best birthday present ever was what's taking place tonight. He's beaten my husband again, and he's piling on the compliments so he can pull the rug out from under Ben. He took my husband's pride and joy, me, and reduced me to a stripper for his pleasure. I had yelled, *"I'm not a whore!"* and he said, *"Maybe not, but you're certainly a stripper."*

Well, when it comes right down to it, it's Roy's word against mine about seeing me naked, and there's no way Ben would believe such a cock-eyed story if I deny it. Ben knows I was out very late Friday night, and that's an issue, but on the bright side I destroyed Carter's cell phone, so there's no photographic evidence. Even if Roy drags Carter Teague in here, it'll be my word against theirs. I'll convince Ben that Roy's trying to put one over on him. I tell myself if it goes down that way I shouldn't act defensively. I need to laugh, or roll my eyes like I would if someone were making up a story about me as a joke. Maybe I'll listen to the whole story, as if spellbound, and say, "Absolutely true. Then I flew back home on my flying unicorn!"

Every now and then, as they're talking, Roy turns to me and gives me a wink. He's a disgusting pig of a man, and I hate myself for being a part of his game. I'm convinced he wants to destroy my husband's faith in me tonight, and I feel sick, cheap and degraded about it. Worse, I feel disloyal to Ben, who's done nothing worse than brag to his old college roommate about how wonderful his wife is.

After dinner, the moment of truth arrives.

Chapter 21

ROY SAYS, "BEN, you've never said a word about my wheelchair."

Ben looks uncomfortable. "Well, I figured you'd explain if you wanted us to know."

"But weren't you even concerned for me?"

"Well, of course I am! But I don't like to intrude."

Roy stares at Ben, enjoying the fact he's making him squirm.

I say, "Tell us, Roy. Why are you sitting in that wheelchair tonight?"

Ben gives me an odd look.

Roy pushes the chair back a few feet and stands up.

Ben's mouth drops.

I clap my hands in a bored, mocking way.

Ben gives me another strange look, and I realize I might be playing right into Roy's hands. So I say, "I knew he was faking the wheelchair."

"Really?" Roy says. "Tell us how!"

"Your hands aren't calloused."

Roy looks at his hands. Ben says, "See? That's what makes her a great private eye!"

"Good for you, Dani," Roy says, none too pleased.

He sits back in the chair and wheels it forward. "The truth is, I'm considering buying the company that makes this particular chair, and I wanted to try it out."

Ben shakes his head with apparent admiration and says, "Who else would do that? This is why you're so successful."

"You might be right," Roy says. "This particular company's in Louisville. Do you ever get to Louisville, Ben?"

"Gosh, it's been a while," Ben says.

Roy turns to me. "How about you, Dani? Does your work ever take you to Louisville?"

I look him in the eye with a steely stare. "Rarely. Why do you ask?"

He holds my gaze and says, "I was there this past weekend."

"Did you wheel yourself all the way here from Louisville?"

He laughs. "You're a saucy little thing, aren't you! Actually, I had this chair waiting for me at the Westin. I've only tested it outside for two blocks, and it wasn't easy. I admire those who use them all the time."

I nod. "Me too."

He says, "Reason I asked about Louisville, I had dinner at Simon Claire's in the Brundage Hotel. Have you tried it?"

Ben says, "We celebrated our anniversary there last year."

"Did you get a room and have wild, passionate sex? Please say yes!"

Ben looks at me.

I say, "Would I be telling too much if I said I could hardly walk the next day?"

Ben smiles, relieved.

Roy, all smiles, says, "So. You're a tiger in bed, are you, Ben?"

Ben shrugs.

Roy says, "Who'd have thought it? Well, good for you guys."

He hands me his cell phone. "I took some pictures of the place. Is it just the way you remembered?"

A cold chill goes through my veins as I take the phone and see the first picture. It's a young blonde sitting in the parlor, face turned downward, texting something on her cell phone. The next picture is a close up of a napkin with red lipstick on it with the words *Call Me!* and a cell phone number.

My cell phone number.

The next four pictures were taken in my hotel room by Carter Teague, who was apparently snapping them from behind me while I was removing my clothes, facing Roy. She caught me in various stages of undress, including my entire naked backside, and sure enough, she even managed to squeeze off a shot of my full frontal nudity before I jumped behind the chair.

It dawns on me if I hadn't turned on the small lamp behind me, these images would have never been visible. It's also clear Carter Teague forwarded the pictures to Roy's phone while I was getting dressed. I destroyed her cell phone, but Roy already had the photos.

His "best birthday present ever" continues.

"Let *me* see," Ben says.

"Shall I share them with Ben?" I ask Roy.

"Your choice," he says, evenly.

"They're a little hard to make out, sweetheart," I say. "Do you have your glasses with you?"

Ben reaches inside his coat pocket for his glasses and puts them on.

"Good!" I say. "Though I'm not sure you'll be overly impressed with the quality. No offense, Roy."

I note the stunned expression on Roy's face before handing his cell phone to Ben.

Chapter 22

BEN SCANS THE pictures and frowns.

"I'm afraid I don't understand," he says.

"They're nude photos of a woman," I say.

Ben places Roy's phone on the table.

"I know *that*," he says. "What I don't understand is why Roy wanted to show them to *you*."

I look at Roy.

"Why *would* you feel comfortable showing me nude pictures of you and a hooker?"

Roy grabs the phone and starts flipping through the photos. What he sees is I've erased the photos of me and left the ones he took of him having sex with Carter Teague after I left. I may not be a successful private eye, but I'm a good one. I know how to get evidence, and how to destroy it. As a plus, even though I'm not a gym rat, I could possibly hold my own against Roy should he decide to throw a punch at me.

"I don't know how you did that," he says angrily, "but this isn't over. Not by a long shot."

Ben and I exchange a look.

"I saw that!" Roy says.

"Sorry," I say, "but you seem upset."

He's more than upset, he's livid.

"Don't celebrate yet, sweet meat. I can still pull the photos from my SIM card."

"I think we've seen enough photos, Roy," Ben says.

"You think, Benny boy? You just wait. You'll see."

In the car, on the way home, Ben says, "Unbelievable."

"What's that?"

"I've never seen him that out of control before. He didn't know how to react."

"I can't believe he'd show me naked pictures of himself," I say, shamelessly.

"Sad to say, that's not out of character for him."

"But why would he *do* that?"

"Ego. He wanted you to see the kind of man you *could* be with instead of me. Did you see the shock on his face when you handed me his cell phone?"

"It was like he got caught flirting with your wife."

"He *was* flirting, and when you showed me his photos it shamed him like he's never been shamed before. In Roy's eyes, losing face in front of *me* is the worst possible insult."

I glance at Ben's face. He's beaming. He catches me looking and says, "I can't thank you enough for tonight. You've done me the biggest favor in the world!"

"How so?"

"Roy calls me a couple of times a year to gloat. Tonight, thanks to you, I've beaten him. Now he knows there's nothing he can say or do to impress me. I expect we'll never hear from him again!"

Ben laughs.

I laugh too, but I have a feeling he's wrong about that.

When we get home, Ben asks if we can have sex.

"I know you're riding a high," I say, "but we have an arrangement, remember?"

"How could I possibly forget the arrangement?" he says. "If you do it now, I'll let you skip my birthday."

This is a good offer. His birthday's a full day. This is a late night quickie.

"You've got yourself a deal," I say.

"How about right here in the kitchen?" he says.

"I'll do it wherever you like. But first I have to pee."

"I'll make it easy on you," he says. "My bed, two minutes."

"Can't wait!" I say, feigning enthusiasm.

I run up the stairs, brush my teeth, toss on a negligee, and catch my reflection in the mirror. Then mouth the words, "Don't look at me like that, Sofe!"

I get almost to the stairs, then run back to my vanity and search till I find the *Daisy, by Marc Jacobs.*

Sophie's perfume.

I dab some on the back of my right hand and make my way down the staircase. When I get to Ben's bedroom, I remind myself to be fun and flirty. He's earned this, and I want to do my very best.

Ben's lovemaking sessions normally last between five and fifteen minutes, depending on whether he's in the mood for three or thirteen minutes of foreplay. But tonight is a whole different ball of wax.

He's doing subtle things to me down there. I put the back of my hand over my mouth and make little pretend whimpers while taking in Sophie's scent. Ben likes the sounds I make, and continues what he's doing, and before I know it, I'm pretending it's Sophie, and he's doing all the things I imagine Sophie doing.

Ben has never approached my body in this manner, and I have to say the little whimpering sounds I'm making are no longer make-believe. I take in Sophie's scent, think of her, and Ben does his thing, and suddenly I'm moving my head back and forth, making sounds I don't recognize. The pleasure's building. I'm breathing faster and faster, my heart's racing, my face is flushed. My back arches, falls and arches again without any help from me. I'm dizzy. I'm euphoric. I'm...I'm about to explode!

Suddenly I yell, "*Give it to me!*"

Huh?

Did I really say that?

Ben's more surprised than I am. But he obliges me. And as he does, I immediately go from physical to mental, which means I no longer feel the flush, the excitement, the sexual engagement. Is it because he's a man?

No.

It's because I confused myself.

Had I been excited thinking of Sophie? Yes. But if so, why did I yell for Ben?

I needed him.

I'm more confused than ever. But not so confused I miss the signals Ben's giving me. He's nearly done, so I make the passionate scunds he's hoping to hear, and let him kiss me. I kiss him back, and touch him in ways that bring him a swift and happy ending. Then I lie in Ben's arms a respectable length of time, kiss him goodnight, trudge up the stairs, climb into my bed, and cry myself to sleep.

Chapter 23

WEDNESDAY MORNING

"THAT'S THE MOST insane thing I've ever heard!" Sophie says.

She's talking about dinner with Roy, not sex with Ben. I haven't told her about Ben, and probably won't. I'm at my real office, not the one at home, and we've been on the phone more than two hours, dissecting every detail of what transpired last night at the restaurant with Roy.

I know lots of women who have guy friends. I have some too, but this is the type of conversation I could never have with them. With guys, you tell them the story, they ask a question or two, you're done. But a girlfriend will ask for the exact wording of each comment, and the tone with which it was spoken. *What did he mean by that?* will be dissected, debated, and analyzed fifteen different ways before

108

the next comment is parsed. It's a matter of layering one detail on top of another, no matter how minute, after factoring in such things as facial expression, nuance, history, wardrobe, eye color, skin tone, bone structure, fragrance, wind velocity, and curvature of the earth.

In the end, Sophie and I have the entire conversation worked out, and it only took us fifteen minutes longer than it took for the events to transpire last night!

"So now you're doing what?" she says.

"Same as always."

"Looking for *ManChild*?"

"Well, he won't be using that name."

"If he's smart enough not to use the name, he's smart enough not to use the phrase."

"The sickest ones are often smart. But when their demons take over, they fall back into familiar patterns of speech."

"I know, but the chances are so slim—"

"*It's all I've got, Sofe!*"

We're both quiet a minute.

"I raised my voice to you," I say.

"I know."

"I'm sorry."

"You had every right," Sophie says. "What you're working on is really important. I don't know how you do it, given what you've been through." She sighs. "I'm supposed to be your friend, supposed to be supportive. And I am, but sometimes my mouth gets in my way."

"It's alright."

We're quiet again, best friends trying to reconnect after an awkward exchange. I feel I should say something, but I'm struggling. Then it comes to me.

"What does the BFF Handbook call for at a time like this?"

"A change of subject."

"Got anything?"

She thinks a minute. "I do. Read me some of the funny posts."

I smile. Sophie's good. She's changing the subject, but keeping me on task. I'll read a couple of perverted posts to her, we'll laugh, hang up. Then I'll dig into the more serious conversation threads that have posted over the last twenty-four hours.

"Ready?" I say.

"Hit me!"

I find one and say, "*PillowLips* says, *I like anagrams. My new online bf said his name is Alan. Do you think that's code for Anal?*"

"She probably thinks Santa is code for Satan."

"Maybe you can work that into a song."

She laughs. "Read me another."

I scan the *Lunatic List* of names I put together to follow on a regular basis. Most are guys, but I keep an eye on a few young ladies in case they turn up missing. The ones I follow are prime candidates.

Sofe says, "What's *FingerSniffer* up to? Gotta love *that* name!"

"Let's see. Nothing since he asked all underage girls to send him *nekkid pix*."

"Did anyone do it?"

"Nope. Or he would've posted."

"Too bad you don't have Carter Teague's photos."

"She's *twice* too old for these men to care."

I read her a couple more, then we hang up.

Ten minutes later, I locate *SeanInPain.*

As expected, *Sean's* post about his younger sister rallied the demons. He's showing forty-six responses! I'm pleased to read that two young ladies are appalled he wants to drug his sister. Unfortunately, forty-four readers are not only encouraging him to do so, they're actually giving him advice. Disturbing advice, including how to acquire date rape drugs, and what he should do to his sister while she's unconscious. *Sean* is grateful. He promises to go through with it as soon as he can score some GHB, which I know to be one of three so-called date rape drugs. Legal with a prescription, GHB is used to treat narcolepsy. In its liquid form, GHB is odorless, colorless, and mixes in alcohol, which intensifies the effect dramatically. *Sean* is taking pre-payments for pictures of her, and I wonder who would trust him to deliver. He says he'll send the four most graphic shots of his fifteen-year-old naked sister for only twenty-five bucks and promises they'll be better than her shower pix.

Shower pix'

The little bastard has taken shower pictures?

I click on the link. And there it is:

Three shower pix of little sister, age 15, highest quality, only $10.00!

I try to remain detached, but the sisterhood gene kicks in and I want to kill him. Since that's not an option, I want to at least warn the poor girl. I nearly sign up, thinking I might obtain a website or mail drop address I can trace back to *Sean*. But then I come to my senses and realize I can't purchase nude photos of underage children! I could go to jail!

I scroll through my cell phone contact list till I come to Patrick Aub. Pat's a policeman. In a moment of weakness (his, not mine) I talked him into giving me what he had on the guy who abducted Jaqui Moreland. It wasn't much, since he wasn't directly involved with the case, but he did know two things: the perp's handle was *ManChild*, and the phrase about the cherrystones had posted on an underage chat site.

Pat answers the phone with, "Dani! Wow, I can't believe you called. Please tell me you found our guy!"

"Not yet."

"But you're still working on it?"

"I'll never stop."

"You're a saint."

"And you're a bullshit artist. And a flirt."

Pat laughs. "Guilty as charged."

Jaqui's mom contacted me two days after the abduction, against the wishes of the local police and FBI. I worked sixty straight hours with no cooperation from law enforcement. The last eight of those hours were logged after the cops found Jaqui's corpse.

I heard about it the same time you did. On TV.

I can understand Jaqui's mom being too upset to call me. But the cops? That was just ugly. Now there's a public rumor the cold case experts are getting involved. I'm thrilled, but I'm not holding my breath on that. If they help, fantastic. If not, I'll keep plugging away. I don't care who gets credit for catching *ManChild*, long as he's put away for good.

Pat says, "Did the Morelands ever pay you for your time?"

"I never asked."

"But they didn't offer?"

"No."

He sighs. "Civilians, right?" He's silent a moment, then says, "Please tell me you and your husband have split!"

"It's not your day, Pat."

"Damn!"

"There's a guy on an underage website, calls himself *SeanInPain*. He could be eighteen, more or less."

"What about him?"

I tell him the story.

Pat says, "You were smart not to order the pictures."

"Can you do something with this?"

"Maybe. It's not my division, but I'll pass the information to Cheryl Goodman. She might be able to authorize purchase of the shower pix and backtrack the transaction."

"Can you put me in the loop?"

"Yeah, I can do that. But if Cheryl finds out..."

"Let's don't tell her."

"Okay."

After ending the call I start a new computer search for *hard and firm as the erection in my pants.*

While the computer loads the references, I stand to stretch my legs. The focal point of my tiny office is the large, single window, and you can't walk more than six steps from any spot without reaching it. I'm standing there now, looking out onto a view of downtown Cincinnati. I'd love to have an office in one of the buildings a block away that overlooks the park square. It's a small park, half a city block, but so much life happens in parks. Kids play, moms meet, lovers hold hands, sit together, kiss, and even propose marriage. The people-watching from my window is limited to sixty feet of street, a coffee shop, a Chinese restaurant, and a discount department store. Instead of seeing people at leisure, like the park view affords, I see people in motion. They're heading east or west, or entering or leaving one of the stores across the street. What stands out for me is anyone who's *not* in motion.

Like the guy directly across the street in front of the coffee shop.

He stands out.

Not only is he motionless, he's looking straight at me. Sees me looking back, and pulls a cell phone from his pocket to make a call. At that very moment my cell phone buzzes on my desk. I let it buzz, content to watch the guy below me, watching me. He points to the phone at his ear.

I walk to the desk, pick up my phone, walk back to the window, and press the button to answer the call.

He says, "We need to talk."

"I don't think so, Roy."

Below me, on the street, he takes the phone away from his ear and stares at it like it's insulting him. Then he puts it back to his ear and says, "I'm coming up."

I click the phone off, cross the room, lock the door.

Then I get my gun.

Chapter 24

"I KNOW YOU'RE in there. Open up or I'll make a scene!" Roy says, trying to keep his voice under control.

"If you make a scene someone will call the police."

"I can talk to you here, or I can come to your home. Which works best for you?"

"Um...here."

I unlock the door and take a few steps back, positioning my gun so it's aimed chest high. Roy opens the door, sees the gun, gasps, and immediately turns sideways and covers up. When he realizes I haven't shot him, he lowers his hands, straightens his stance, and says, "Are you *nuts? Jeez!*"

"I don't like you."

"Relax, will you?"

"I don't like you."

"So you said. Put the gun down, okay? We both know you're not going to shoot me."

"What do you want?"

"Would you put the freaking gun away? You're making me nervous."

I'm making *me* nervous, too. I've never shot anyone before, and don't want to start now. But I'm highly agitated, and my shoulders are shaking. Soon it'll be my hands.

"Sit on the couch," I say, "but keep your hands where I can see them."

He does, and I close the door while keeping the gun pointed at him.

"Dani," he says.

"What?"

"The gun?"

"The gun stays where it is. You threatened to *rape* me."

"We weren't serious about that."

"Says you."

He sighs.

"Can you at least take your finger off the trigger?"

"Yeah, I can do that."

I place my finger outside the trigger guard and sit behind my desk, facing him. I keep the gun pointed at his chest, but rest the base of the grip on the desk to steady it. Now if he comes at me, it'll be impossible to miss him.

He knows it, I know it.

"Where's your wife?"

He shakes his head. "Carter's not my wife."

"Your girlfriend?"

"Not any more."

"What did you want to talk about, Roy?"

"How did you erase the photos? They aren't even on the memory stick."

"Memory stick?"

"SIM card. Whatever."

"I'm afraid that's a trade secret. Was there anything else?"

"Yeah."

"Go ahead."

'I came here to warn you," he says

"You warned me last night."

"Huh?"

"'This isn't over,' you said. 'Not by a long shot.'"

"That wasn't me. That was the bourbon."

"Uh huh. But now you've got a different warning for me?"

"That's right. I'm going to make you famous. Would you like that?"

"You want to be my publicist?"

He smiles. "Let's talk about you and Benny."

"What about us?"

"Ever wonder how your paths crossed?"

"What do you know about our paths?"

"I never put it together till now."

I frown. "Roy, look at me. According to Ben you're some sort of business mogul. Is that true? Are you in fact a successful businessman?"

"Of course! I'm worth millions."

"Then will you do me the honor of talking in complete sentences? You sound like that old cop show on TV, where everyone talks in staccato."

"Which one?"

"What difference does it make? Just tell me, all at once, what you came here to say."

"*Dragnet.*"

"What?"

"The TV show you're talking about. *Dragnet.* 'Just the facts, ma'am.' I'm right, right?"

"I don't know. I'm twenty-four years old. I saw it on some show where comedians were making fun of old TV shows."

"*Dragnet* was a classic. They had these two detectives—"

"Roy!"

"Huh?"

"Enough about the TV show."

He shrugs his shoulders and says, "You're the one brought it up."

I speak to him slowly, as if talking to a small child. "Roy. For the love of God. Will you please tell me what you came here to say?"

"I think you might be the little girl they pulled out of that crazy guy's basement a few years back."

I wasn't expecting *that* bombshell, and he can tell I wasn't. I have to regroup, and fast. I force myself to look puzzled instead of shocked. "I have no idea what you're talking about."

"Mindy Renee Whittaker."

"Wait. You think *I'm* her?"

"That's right."

I shake my head and laugh, but it doesn't sound convincing, even to me. So I add, "That's ridiculous!"

"You sure about that?"

"Quite."

"Where are you from, originally?"

"Pittsburgh."

He frowns. "Pittsburgh?"

"Roy?"

"Yeah?"

"You're doing that *Dragnet* thing again."

"Maybe so, but I think you're her."

I sigh. "The girl you're talking about is from Portland, not Pittsburgh. And they didn't drag her out of a basement, she broke free and walked into a precinct house. From what I've seen on TV, the media wouldn't leave her alone. The police feared for her safety, so they put her and her mother in witness protection and relocated her somewhere."

"Cincinnati's somewhere."

"Oh. Well, you've got me there, Roy," I say with great sarcasm. "Yes, you're absolutely correct. Cincinnati *is* somewhere."

"You get all your information from TV?" he says.

"Pretty much. But just for the sake of argument, what led you to draw this absurd conclusion?"

"Your husband, Benny."

"What about him?"

"He was fascinated with her. No, fascinated isn't the right word. He was *obsessed*."

"What are you *talking* about?"

He sweeps his hand indicating a wide area and says, "It was all over the news. For weeks. Biggest search party ever."

"So?"

"Around the time all that was going on I called Benny, to tell him what I was up to. You know, all my business and personal conquests." He winks. Then says, "During that call he said he was going to meet that little girl and marry her someday. I called him a pedophile, and he hung up on me."

I try to keep my expression neutral, but it's hard to do with ice crystals forming in my veins. Also, my stomach is acting funny.

I swallow.

When I'm able to speak with a steady voice, I say, "Pedophilia refers to adults attracted to prepubescent children, not fifteen-year-olds. In any case, Ben didn't marry Mindy Renee, he married me."

He stares at my face as if trying to memorize it for a quiz.

"Maybe," he says. "But he did manage to meet her when she was seventeen. He even got a job tutoring her."

"He told you that?"

"You're pretending you don't know any of this?"

"I'm not pretending," I say. "The whole idea's insane."

It is insane. My mom called Ben from an ad he put up at the grocery store. At least that's the story I heard. But did I hear that from Mom? Or Ben?

Roy says, "The next time I called Ben, he said Mindy Renee was nuts, and he quit tutoring her to take a teaching job at Clifton State. A few months later, he turns up married to you. I didn't think much about it till I saw you last week. When I saw how young you were and thought about Ben tapping that fine ass of yours, I remembered how Ben was obsessed with that little girl. She was also blonde."

"He was probably concerned for her welfare."

Roy laughs, but it comes out ugly. "Is it true what they said about how you escaped?"

"It wasn't me. I have no idea if her story is true. I sincerely doubt it."

He looks at me like he's sizing me up. Then says, "Your sweet Ben was creaming his jeans to get the tutoring job. When he got it he couldn't stop bragging. A few months later little Mindy Renee disappears and changes her name and Ben marries a blonde happens to be the same age."

"You're repeating yourself."

"Doesn't make me wrong."

"Actually, you *are* wrong. Mindy Renee changed her name shortly after escaping. She and her mother went into witness protection to escape being harassed by the media. She was fifteen. Witness protection has a one hundred percent success rate. It's never been breached. So I doubt Ben tracked her down at age seventeen. And I doubt Mindy and her mom ever relocated to Cincinnati."

He flashed a smug smile. "You sure seem to know a lot about it."

"I'm a private investigator. I know how witness protection works."

"Ben never said her new name. Just that it was the same girl. And he never said he tracked her down."

"Then what *did* he say, Roy?"

"He said Mindy and her mom moved to Cincinnati, and in an incredible stroke of freak luck, Mindy's mom—*your* mom—contacted *him*. About a tutoring job. And even though he signed some sort of secrecy agreement, he couldn't keep from bragging to his old pal, Roy."

"Let's see if I've got this straight," I say. "You're warning me that Ben had a creepy obsession for Mindy Renee Whittaker, and through dumb luck got a job tutoring her, but found her crazy. So he met me and decided I'd be her replacement? Is that your warning? That Ben wasn't in love with me when we got married? Or are you warning me you think Ben's a hebephile?"

"I don't even know what that is," he says.

"An adult who's attracted to children in the early years of puberty. Is that your warning, Roy?"

"No. My warning's more specific."

"Can you just give it and go?"

"When the world finds out you're Mindy Renee Whittaker your life will never be the same."

"Roy."

"Yes, hon?" he says, in a mocking tone.

"Why on earth would the world think I'm Mindy Renee Whittaker?"

"Because I'm going to leak the story to the tabloids."

I force a chuckle. "You're going to end up looking stupid if you do "

"I'm willing to take my chances."

"If you're dead set on doing it, why haven't you done it already?"

"I wanted to tell you first."

"Why?"

"To watch you sweat."

Chapter 25

"ROY?"

"Yeah?"

"Can I ask you a question?"

"Of course."

"What really happened between you and Ben?"

"What do you mean?"

"You've been calling him for years, bragging, flaunting your success in his face. You spent a small fortune and went to a great deal of effort to set me up through Carter Teague. You didn't go to all this trouble because you're competitive. Ben obviously did something to you, years ago. Or at least, you think he did."

"Ask Ben."

I frown. "What are we, in junior high? Ben will have his own version, if he says anything at all. I'd like to hear your side."

He says, "I'll make you a deal. Tell me how you erased the photos from my cell phone and I'll tell you the truth about what Ben did to me."

"Carter sent the photos to your cell phone," I say.

"So?"

"Since you didn't take the photos from *your* phone, there was no memory of them. I didn't have to erase them from your SIM card, I only had to delete them from your inbox. For example, I couldn't have erased the pictures you took of you and Carter after I left, because those were taken by your phone."

"And they'd be in the memory chip somewhere."

"In a manner of speaking."

He nods. "You're not stupid."

"Sometimes I am."

"He cost me a scholarship."

"What?"

"Ben. He cost me a football scholarship."

"How?"

"I used to play practical jokes on him. Nothing major, just funny, you know?"

"Funny to you."

He shrugs. "Whatever. Anyway, one night he found me passed out on my bed and decided to play one on me. He wrapped twine around me, tying me to the bed. Then he hung my alarm clock from the ceiling so it was inches from my ear."

"Sounds harmless enough."

"Except this was the night before the away game with Georgia Tech, and the alarm clock was set for five a.m. And when Ben was screwing around with it, he somehow turned the alarm off by mistake. I woke up at eight the next morning and missed the bus."

"Why didn't someone call you?"

"College kids didn't have cell phones back then. To make matters worse, the kid who replaced me played the best game of his life. Six weeks later our team went to the Independence Bowl, and the coach started him instead of me. The game was close, and I had to watch from the bench. I was a junior. That was my first and last bowl game, because the coach pulled my scholarship."

He's staring off into space, reliving it. I remain quiet until he speaks.

"I'll never forgive him for that," he says. "Never."

I nod. "That's a big thing."

"Ya think?"

"Yes. But you said it yourself. He turned the alarm off by mistake."

"What if I killed Ben by mistake? Would you forgive me?"

"Not at first, probably. But eventually? Yes, I think so."

He gives me a doubtful expression.

I shrug. "I can't guarantee it," I say, "but I like to think that after all this time—"

"Well, you're obviously a better person than me," he says.

I note the disgust in his voice. "I'm sorry for what happened, Roy."

"No need for *you* to be sorry, Mindy."

I sigh. "I'm not Mindy. But I *am* sorry. Sorry for what Ben did to you all those years ago, and sorry you feel the need to punish him through me. But here's what I don't understand. Say I *am* Mindy Renee, and you make it public knowledge. How does that punish Ben?"

He shrugs. "When I hurt you, I hurt Ben."

"You'd do that to me, knowing what I went through?"

He smiles. "You mean, hypothetically?"

"Of course."

"The answer is yes. I'd do that to you in a heartbeat."

"Why?"

"Because I don't give a shit what happens to you."

"Okay then."

"Okay what?"

"Go sell your story."

"Would you like to know what it would take to keep me quiet?"

"No."

"Really?"

"Really. I'm not Mindy Renee, so your revelation won't affect me in the least."

He points to the gun. "Am I free to go?"

I lay the gun sideways on my desktop, but hold it just in case. He chuckles, then gets up and leaves. I wait ten minutes to make certain he isn't standing in the hallway, then I put my head on my desk and sob like I haven't sobbed in years.

Chapter 26

"JEREDITH," I SAY, "This is..."

Dillon gives me a look.

"This is what?" Jeredith says.

"Captain Spaceship," I say.

Dillon bows.

"You're a captain?"

"That's right," Dillon says. "Captain Spaceship."

"What branch of the military?"

Dillon sneers. "What do you mean, *branch?*"

Jeredith frowns. "I'd cut that hair off if you were in my barracks, mister. And I wouldn't give a rat's ass about your rank, neither. I'd do it in the middle of the night. Put some bars of lye soap in a burlap bag, and smack you in the head, and knock your ass out. Then I'd cut that nasty hair off your filthy head!"

"You got any Lucky Charms?" Dillon says.

Jeredith looks at me and says, "Is he retarded?"

"Dillon likes to eat sugary cereal while he works."

"I'm a tweaker, man," he says.

"You'll fire up no crystal meth in *my* house," Jeredith says. "Nor snort it."

Dillon and I look at her in total confusion.

She says, "I know what tweeking is. I watch cop shows on TV."

I look at Dillon.

He says, "That's tweeker with two e's. I'm a tweaker with an a."

Jeredith gives me a look.

"He's brilliant," I say. "He just loves his sugar."

"You," she says to Dillon, giving him a wary look.

"What?"

"Stay out of my pantry. I won't be a party to your addiction."

She stands aside to let us enter the house. To our left is a small dining room. To our right, an office.

"Is that Burt's computer?" I say.

"Try not to leave evidence," she says.

Dillon parks himself in Burt's chair and fires up the computer. Jeredith and I head to her kitchen to chat. We sit at her table and talk a few minutes.

At one point she asks, "Where are your people from?"

Before I finish answering, Dillon joins us, holding a sheet of paper in his hand. In a very matter-of-fact voice, he says, "Burt's fucking Amy."

I glare at him while saying, "Jeredith, I have to apologize for Dillon's lack of tact."

She says nothing.

"Do you know an Amy?" I say.

"Only Amy I know is his Aunt Amy. But she's eighty-two."

Dillon says, "Amy Lattimore?"

Jeredith frowns. "That'd be Aunt Amy."

To Dillon I say, "You're sure?"

"They're at her place right now."

"They're probably just visiting," I say.

Dillon starts to read from the page he's printed from Burt's computer:

Amy, I can't wait to see you today! Do you have any lube left? I hope so, because I'm going to pork you six ways to Sunday! Just make sure your teeth are out before you—"

"Thanks, Dillon!" I say. "We've heard enough."

I ask Jeredith if she wants to confront Aunt Amy and her husband.

"A' course I do!"

"Would you like us to be there?"

"You'll *have* to be there," she says. "I don't have a car."

"We can drive you," I say.

"Go start the car," she says. "I'll get my shotgun."

Chapter 27

"JEREDITH! YCU CAN'T bring a weapon!"

"What?"

"You can't bring a weapon!"

"Well, how the hell am I supposed to kill 'em without a weapon?"

"You don't *kill* them, you divorce *him*."

"That's the dumbest thing I ever heard! You'd have me give what little money we got to a damn *attorney*?"

Dillon says, 'Can I get paid now?"

I look at Jeredith. "If you kill them, you'll go to prison."

She says, "If you won't let me take the shotgun, I reckon I'll have to quietly poison him when he gets home."

I hold up my hand. "Why would you say that to me?"

"Are you going to tell?"

"Yes, of course!"

She frowns. "How much do I owe you?"

"How does a hundred sound?"

"Like ninety dollars too much."

"Make it sixty," I say.

"Fifty-five," she says. "And a box of Sugar Smacks for the kid."

I look at Dillon.

"I don't know what that is," he says, "but I like the sound of it."

Jeredith counts out fifty-five dollars, hands it to me, and heads to the pantry. I pass the money to Dillon.

Now in the car, I check my phone and see three voice mail messages. Sometimes I go a whole day without getting three. I put my ear buds in and listen to them. Then see Dillon staring at me.

"What?"

He says, "Is it all about sex?"

"What are you talking about?"

"PI work."

"Yeah, pretty much. For me, at least."

"Do you ever get paid?"

"Not for PI work."

He stares at the crumpled bills in his hand like he's making a major decision. Finally he says, "I'll give you fifty for a blow job."

I laugh, try to stop, then laugh some more.

"What's so funny?

"Eat your cereal, Dillon."

Chapter 28

THE FIRST TWO voice messages are from Sophie. I'd called her on my way to pick up Dillon, but she'd been working on a song and didn't hear the phone. When she got my voice message she could tell I'd been crying, and wanted to console me. Hell of a friend, Sophie. The third message was from Janice Uvula, an attorney who said we met at a wedding reception a few months ago. I don't remember Janice, but she said I made a good impression. She also said she left a subpoena with her secretary, if I want to deliver it.

I call the secretary.

"Conner, Palate, Tonsil, and Uvula. This is Donna. How may I help you today?"

I tell her.

Donna gives me the address and says she'll supply the details when I come to her office. I punch the address into my GPS and realize how close I am.

"I can be there in five minutes," I say.

We hang up. Dillon groans.

"Quit griping. You're still on the clock."

"That's bogus!"

"Bogus? What does *that* mean?"

"It means I've been paid. Which means my job is done."

I start the car and ease out of the driveway, so my GPS system can guide me to Janice's office. "You're free to walk home," I say. "It's only what, twelve miles? Otherwise, indulge me."

"How long?"

"Five minutes to the attorney's office, five more inside. I'll have you home in thirty minutes, tops."

He frowns.

"Look," I say. "This might be an actual PI job."

"Not related to sex?"

"Possibly not. Anyway, it's my first job for an attorney. If I don't screw it up, I might get some regular work."

"This could be your big break?"

"Not even close. But it could be *something*."

Within minutes I'm pulling in the parking lot.

Dillon says, "You getting paid?"

"I am."

"How much?"

"She didn't say."

"Uh huh."

He breaks open the Sugar Smacks and starts eating.

I wince, then ask, "What's the sugar content of that cereal?"

"I dunno. Why?"

"The smell makes my teeth itch!"

"Want some?"

I shake my head, put the car in park.

"Stay here," I say. "I'll be right back."

"Five minutes," he says. "Or I'll come in and embarrass you."

I flip him the finger and exit the car.

Janice Uvula's office is on the ground floor of the Kotter-Banks Legal & Medical Center, a four-story concrete structure featuring a large, airy lobby and a beautiful turquoise-blue brick floor. The bricks have some sort of shiny glaze on them, which seems insane, since anyone in black, silver-studded ankle boots with four-inch heels, like I'm wearing, could slip, take a nasty tumble, and crawl in any direction to be treated for the injury, then limp in any other direction to file the lawsuit. But though my narrow heels click and reverberate through the lobby as I walk, the surface has adequate traction, and I arrive at Janice's office without incident.

After I introduce myself, Donna has me fill out some paperwork. When I hand it back to her she says, "We pay seventy-five dollars for service of process."

"That seems fair," I say.

She gives me one of those all-encompassing looks where her eyes go from my face to my body to my ankle boots and back up to my face again. I get the feeling my wardrobe is telling her something about me.

She says, "Have you ever served a subpoena before?"

"Only in PI school."

"PI school?"

"I took a training class."

She nods, but looks skeptical. "You're aware there are two types?"

"One is for people, the other's for physical evidence, right?"

She looks at me the way my ninth-grade geometry teacher, Mrs. Moody, used to look at me when I got the answer right but couldn't recite the formula.

"That's essentially accurate," Donna says.

Mrs. Moody said I'd never survive in the real world without a thorough understanding of geometry, so I spent hours every night studying, and wound up getting an A. That summer, when Colin Tyler Hicks chloroformed me, threw me in his van, and locked me in the basement of his farm house, I learned the hard way Mrs. Moody was full of shit. Geometry had nothing to do with my survival.

"Which type of subpoena will I be delivering today?" I ask.

"*Ad Testificandum.*"

"Which type will I be delivering today?" I repeat.

She frowns. "*Ad Testificandum* orders a person to testify before the ordering authority. You'll need to identify yourself as a representative of Conner, Palate, Tonsil, and Uvula, and place the subpoena directly into the hands of one William DeWitt."

"What's he done?"

Donna frowns again, and it strikes me that women seem to frown a lot in my presence.

She says, "What Mr. DeWitt has or hasn't done is really none of your concern, is it?"

I shrug, take the subpoena, and say, "Is there anything I need to know about Mr. DeWitt?"

"Just his address," she says. "It's not brain surgery, Dani."

"Maybe not, but it seems awfully easy for seventy-five dollars."

"Mrs. Uvula bills her clients five hundred an hour, so she's ahead of the game hiring someone to do it. Plus, she likes you. Do a good job, and you'll probably become our go-to process server."

I like the sound of that.

"Anything else?" I say.

"Just call me when you've delivered the subpoena, and make a note of the date, time, and circumstances, in case you need to testify."

"Testify?"

"Don't worry, it won't come to that. But you do need to have documentation."

I set my jaw.

"I won't let you down," I say.

She rolls her eyes. "It's just handing a guy a piece of paper, Dani."

"Still."

"Fine. I'll let Mrs. Uvula know she can count on you."

I salute.

"To the bitter end," I say.

"Dani?"

"Yes?"

"Go serve the paper."

"Okay."

Chapter 29

BACK IN THE car, Dillon says, "You were in there twelve minutes."

"No way."

He holds up a stopwatch to prove it.

"Are you kidding me?"

"I clicked it when you closed the car door," he says, "clicked it again just now."

"Your parents must be so proud."

"My parents are morons."

I decide a subject change is in order.

"Want to go with me to deliver a subpoena?"

"*Ad testificandum* or *duces tecum*?"

Eyeing him closely, I say, "The first one."

He laughs. "You can't even pronounce it, can you?"

I work it out in my head, but decide it's not going to come out of my mouth accurately.

"I don't need to pronounce it, I just need to deliver it."

"Man or woman?"

"Man."

"Home or business?"

"Home."

"What's the address?"

I tell him.

"That's not far," he says. "What're they paying you, a hundred?"

"Seventy-five."

"I'll go with you for half."

"I'll give you ten dollars."

He frowns. "Twenty."

"Have a heart, Dillon. I got nothing from Jeredith."

"That's not my fault."

I sigh. "Okay."

His face brightens. "Okay as in you'll pay me the twenty?"

"Okay as in I'll take you home and deliver the subpoena myself."

I put the car in gear and exit the parking lot. We get about a mile and Dillon says, "I'll go with you for ten."

"Don't do me any favors," I say, huffily.

"You don't know what's behind that door," he says. "You'll be safer with me there."

I glance at him, wondering if he's being sincere. Dillon's eighteen, with industrial strength acne and long, greasy hair he keeps in a pony tail. He's six-three, thin as a rail, and has the type of build that, if he were athletic, his teammates would call him *Stretch*. But he's not athletic, he's a computer

140

nerd. Smart enough to be a forensic investigator, skilled enough to hack the Pentagon, but socially inept. He seems sincere.

"I'll make it fifteen," I say. "We'll go in together."

"Deal."

Fifteen minutes later I pull into William DeWitt's driveway. William lives in a tiny, one-story ranch in dire need of a paint job. The left side of his carport is caved in. An old, rusty Nash Rambler sits on cinder blocks in the right side, directly in front of us.

"Wonder if he'd sell the car," Dillon says.

"You can ask him, if you like."

I park the car, hand Dillon fifteen bucks, note the time, 2:23 p.m., and the weather. Sunny, warm, few clouds.

"Ready?"

He nods.

"Let's roll!"

We get out of the car and start walking toward the front door. Dillon looks at me and says, "I thought you went to PI school."

"I did."

"Hide the papers."

"What?"

"He'll never let you in if he thinks you're going to serve him papers."

I look at the paperwork in my hands.

"I knew that," I say.

I walk back to the car, put the papers in my handbag. By then, Dillon's already on the doorstep. As I approach, carrying the handbag, I hear music, and a woman's voice shouting instructions. Dillon turns toward me with a disgusted look on his face.

"What's the matter?" I say.

He puts his finger to his lips, indicating me to be quiet. Then motions me to join him on the concrete slab that serves as a doorstep.

I do, and whisper, "What's wrong?"

He points to the screen door, but I can't see inside from my vantage point.

Dillon whispers, "Do this," and puts his hands on either side of his head, to shield his eyes while looking through the screen. Then turns to me and whispers, "It's always about sex with you."

I frown, shield my eyes the way he did, and look inside.

Chapter 30

THE MAN I assume to be William DeWitt is standing in his living room facing his television. He's watching an exercise program, trying to follow the moves called out by the female fitness guru. But William is enormously fat, the fattest human I've ever seen, and appears only capable of shifting his weight from side to side, while pawing the air with his arms in a way that bears little similarity to the action taking place on the TV screen.

Oh, and William is completely naked, save for the silver chandelier earrings that hang a full eight inches from his ear lobes.

The earrings are getting a better workout than William.

Dillon and I look at each other, and I start laughing.

DeWitt hears me, and turns to look. He squeals, and rushes to turn off the TV. Then he comes to the door and starts to unlatch it, but changes his mind.

"Are you here to serve me papers?" he says.

Dillon and I look at each other.

"If you are, I'll let you in. You, Blondie, not him."

"I'll have to insist that my friend comes in with me," I say.

DeWitt frowns. "He can come in, but he has to stand by the door at all times. Those are my terms."

I look at Dillon for the third time. He says, "This is the business you chose to embrace."

"Are you William DeWitt?" I say.

"I am."

I lock my eyes on his and tell myself *No matter what happens, don't look below his chin. If you do, your head will burst into flames!*

I take a deep breath and say, "I'm Dani Ripper. On behalf of Conner, Palate, Tonsil, and Uvula law firm, I hereby serve notice you must appear before the court. The details regarding your court appearance can be found in these papers."

I remove the papers from my handbag and hold them against the screen door so he can view them.

He unlatches the door and backs up ten feet. I open it, and Dillon enters first. I follow him inside and close the screen door behind me.

"You," he says to Dillon, "Stay where you are and don't move. You," he says to me, "Roll the papers up and place them in my hand."

I roll the papers so they resemble the cardboard tube that's left when all the paper towels are gone. I take a few steps toward him, extending the papers, but DeWitt puts his hands behind his back and giggles. Each time I approach him, he turns his body so I can't get to his hands. I make a couple of attempts, and he grins and says, "Serve me, Blondie! Serve me!"

I feint to the right, try to slide around him to the left, but he hops and spins and manages to keep his front to me at all times.

I frown.

"Dani?" Dillon says.

"Yeah?"

"You don't have to actually place the papers in his hand."

"I don't?"

"No. You've identified yourself, revealed your purpose, and whom you represent."

I look at him. "Did you just say 'whom?'"

He shrugs. "I don't know if it's whom or who. But either way, put the papers on the table, and consider him served."

"You're an *asshole!*" DeWitt says to Dillon.

I put the papers on the end table by the sofa and say, "William DeWitt?"

"Yeah?"

"Consider yourself served."

"Fuck you both!"

In the car, on the way to Dillon's house, I say, "Why didn't you tell me that sooner?"

"About the papers? I was having fun watching you dance with the naked guy."

We ride awhile and he says, "Did you see the size of his nuts?"

"His *what?*"

Dillon laughs.

"I most certainly did *not!*" I say.

We ride some more in silence. Then I ask, "Why? Was there something wrong with them?"

"His nuts?"

He pauses a minute, then says, "You ever go to the state fair?"

"Sure. Why?"

"Ever visit the livestock area?"

"I love the animals."

"Ever see the sheep?"

"Of course. Why?"

Then it hits me.

"Eew!"

"Not the ewes," he says. "The rams. DeWitt's balls were purple, and looked exactly like the nuts on the rams at the fair."

"Thanks for sharing," I say.

"Are you going to sit there and tell me you never look at their private parts?"

"On the *sheep?*"

"The sheep, the goats, the bulls, horses, dogs, men..."

"No."

We go silent until we enter his neighborhood. Then Dillon says, "Does your husband know?"

"Know what?"

"That you're bisexual?"

Chapter 31

"WHAT?"

"It's okay. I'm cool with it."

I give him a look. "Why would you say that?"

"It's obvious."

"How?"

He starts to say something, then stops. "Let's just change the subject," he says.

I say, "Is it because I don't stare at animal dicks?"

He says nothing.

"Is it because of DeWitt? Could you possibly think all hetero women would want to look at that poor man's genitals today?"

Dillon says nothing.

"William DeWitt's a sad case," I say. "He's obviously disturbed. I can't believe *you'd* stare at his private area! What does that say about *you*?"

I turn into his driveway.

"Oh, wait!" I say. "Is it because I wouldn't blow you for fifty bucks? Is that it? Well, here's a question for you. Your mother's hetero. Would *she* blow you for fifty bucks?"

"No need to get hostile," he says.

I park the car and shake my head.

"It's nothing to be ashamed of," he says. "Hell, I'm still a *virgin*."

"I'm not ashamed," I say. "I mean, I wouldn't be ashamed. Either way."

He starts to say something, but I interrupt him.

"Whatever I am, it's none of your business!" I say. "And certainly not the sort of information I'd share with *you*, in any case."

"I just told you I'm a *virgin!*"

"So?"

"Do you have any idea how hard that is to admit?"

"I would think you'd be proud."

"*Proud? It's humiliating!*"

"Well, that's ridiculous."

He gives me a look. "That's all you've got to say?"

"No. Don't forget your cereal."

Dillon's lower lip trembles and I remember he's still something of a child, emotionally. He's about to cry. That happens sometimes, when emotionally-challenged young men find themselves in the presence of a complete and utter bitch. He opens the door to leave, but continues sitting in my car. I think he's waiting for the apology I owe him. Then again, this is Dillon we're talking about, and he might be lingering because he hates his home life.

I've had a rough day, what with Roy threatening to blow my cover and ruin my life. I'm frustrated, angry, and scared. And feel completely helpless, knowing Roy's in control of my future happiness. I'm also sexually confused. Confused about how I felt with Sophie Monday night. Confused about how I felt with Ben last night. Confused about what Dillon just said to me. Am I bisexual? Or just hopelessly screwed up because of what Colin Tyler Hicks did to me in that basement nine years ago?

And what I did to him, in order to escape.

I shake the gruesome thoughts from my mind and start my apology.

"Dillon? You were great today, at DeWitt's house."

"Damn right I was," he sniffs.

"I was lucky you were with me."

"Whatever."

"I acted like a bitch. I'm sorry."

"What are you, on the rag or something?"

I frown. "That's your first thought? Can't I just be having a bad day?"

"You never have bad days."

I cock my head and look at him. For the second time today he seems completely sincere.

"Dillon?"

"Yeah?"

"That may be the nicest thing anyone's ever said to me."

"You're welcome...shit bitch."

I laugh. Then say, "I'm sorry to hear you're a virgin."

"You probably already knew."

"I had no idea!"

Of course I knew. Dillon could spend the night in a whorehouse with hundred dollar bills taped to his boxers and not get laid.

He remains in the car, but shuts the door and looks at me.

"It's embarrassing," he says.

"All your buds are getting laid?"

"Buds?"

"Don't be haughty. You know what I mean."

"Yeah. They're all getting laid. A *lot*."

"Maybe they're lying."

"No, they're definitely scoring."

He sighs and goes quiet, and fiddles with the plastic cup holder between our seats.

I say, "Want some advice?"

He looks at me. "Real advice?"

I nod. "I see three flaws in your game."

"That's pretty harsh."

"Think of it this way. You're only three steps away from getting laid."

"Of course, you're a lot older," he says, "so your advice might be stone age."

I shrug.

He adds, "Then again, you're a babe."

"My advice is universal among babes of all ages. You want to hear it?"

"Yeah, go ahead."

"Hygiene, wardrobe, communication."

He frowns. "I bathe."

"Twice a day?"

150

"Twice a *day*?"

"Yes, and clear up the face. Get your mom to take you to a dermatologist. There are tons of products. Creams, lotions, pills...and dermabrasion to get rid of the acne scars."

"That'll take years!"

"Months."

"Still, that's a long time."

"The time's going to pass either way. May as well have clean, healthy skin and a girlfriend."

"*Girlfriend?*"

"You don't want a girlfriend?"

"Nah, I'll probably play the field," he says.

I work to hold back a smile.

"What's wrong with my wardrobe? And remember, you're old."

"Older, not old. And your clothes are babe proof."

"What's that mean?"

"Like someone dressed you with babe repellent."

"That's bogus!"

"Dillon, a change is in order. It starts with your hygiene, but the whole package needs an upgrade. And by the way, I'm not finished with the hygiene."

"Jesus, you sound like my mom."

"Thank you so much for that. Communication's number three on the list, and that's no small issue with you. But hygiene is more than showers and clean skin. It's hair. Nails. Breath. Diet."

"*Diet?*"

"If you and I were going on a three day road trip and you could bring four things, what would you bring?"

"Four boxes of condoms."

"I guess I'll take that as a compliment, though it sounds rather ambitious."

"Says you."

"Four things to eat, Dillon. What would you bring on the hypothetical trip? Four types of sugary cereal?"

"I'd take cereal, sure. For *one* of my food groups. I mean, who wouldn't? After all, breakfast is the most important meal of the day! But I'm eclectic. I'd take other things."

"Such as?"

"Chicken fingers, French fries, cookie cake..."

"Sounds like a six-year-old kid's birthday menu."

He frowns. "If I make all these changes, I wouldn't be me."

We look at each other without speaking.

Then he says, "Getting laid might not be worth the hassle."

"That's been my experience so far," I say.

"Maybe you haven't met the right woman yet," he says.

Chapter 32

DINNER WITH BEN.

We're home, and he ordered Chinese without checking with me. All these years and he still doesn't know what I like, so he over-ordered. There must be ten containers on the kitchen table, and twenty packets of soy sauce, which I don't use.

The food odor is strong, but I'm picking up a different scent.

"Did someone stop by today?" I ask.

"What do you mean?"

"A woman."

"Why would you think that?"

"I'm smelling perfume."

"It's probably the sweet and sour sauce."

I give him a look.

"What?"

"You think I can't tell the difference between perfume and sweet and sour sauce?"

He shakes his head like I'm crazy. Maybe I am, but this is a scent I recognize. Someone I know wore it recently. But who? Vicky Stringfellow? Carter Teague? Wouldn't it be funny if Vicky left our lunch date all indignant, but then contacted Ben? I wonder if she sat on this very couch and flirted with him. Did she kiss him?

I poke around till I find some won ton soup, lift the lid, and stir it with one of the plastic spoons they provided with the order. As a cloud of steam rises above the soup, I wonder if the spoon will melt if I keep stirring. Then I wonder if the Styrofoam container might leach chemicals into the broth. I look up to see Ben grinning at me.

"What?"

"You were wild last night," he says. Then—I'm not making this up—he winks at me!

"It was nice," I say.

"*Nice*? It was *fantastic*! Best sex we ever had, by far!"

I keep stirring my soup. If it doesn't cool off soon I'll probably put an ice cube in it.

"Don't you agree?" he says.

"Huh?"

I fill the spoon with soup and put it to my mouth. It's still steaming, so I blow on it gently, and say "Thanks for taking care of dinner tonight."

"My pleasure."

"That was really nice of you."

I swallow the soup and wince at the temperature, then pick up the entire container and blow on it. It's so hot it makes my hand uncomfortable just holding it.

Ben says, "Was last night the best sex you ever had?"

I feel like setting my hair on fire and running from the room. Why must he keep going on and on about last night? A few of the minutes were nice. But I also cried myself to sleep afterward.

I know what he wants to hear: *Last night was the best sex of my life, Ben! Wow, what a lover YOU turned out to be! You're like a god in the bedroom, and I can't wait till the next session!* But I don't want to encourage him. I see him looking at me, waiting for an answer. What was it he asked? Was last night the best sex I ever had? I shrug and say, "I guess."

Ben says, "I never heard you cry out like that before. And the way you touched me toward the end—"

"Ben?"

"Yes?"

"Can we not talk about last night?"

"Why?"

"It's weird talking about it the next day."

"You're embarrassed?"

"A little."

"I don't understand. You're a woman. You're supposed to want to talk about everything. Especially relationships. Here I'm trying to talk about our relationship. Last night was a very happy surprise and I was hoping you had a great time too."

"You weren't asking about us having a great time, you were asking if we had great sex."

"What's the difference?"

"Seriously?"

He thinks a minute while we eat. "Okay," he says. "I can understand how the two might be different things to you. But I was having a great time *during* sex, and it seemed you were, too."

"I was."

"So you weren't pretending," he says.

"Of course not."

"Okay, then."

"But that doesn't mean I want to talk about it the next day."

"That's the part I don't get."

I sigh. "Sex is an in-the-moment thing. If I start thinking you're going to review and critique my every move the next day, I'll probably just lie there like a statue next time."

He sets his jaw angrily and says, "Thank you so much."

"I don't understand your tone."

"You just managed to suck all the fun out of last night."

I put the soup container back on the table and stare at the man I've lived with all these years, the one who's angry because I gave him the best sex of his life last night. I pleased him so much we're actually *fighting* about it tonight? Does *that* make sense? And am I really expected to apologize for hurting his feelings over the fact I don't want to rehash every gasp, shudder, and moan I made? Is there a Guinness category for how many apologies a person has made in a day? Because I may be closing in on it. In the last eight hours I've apologized to Sophie, Roy, and Dillon. And now Ben? Well, why the hell not?

"I'm sorry," I say. "I've had a shit day. That's my only excuse."

"What happened?"

"Let's just try to enjoy dinner and put this day behind us, okay?"

"Fine."

Moments later Ben grabs his lower stomach and runs to the bathroom.

"Don't eat the moo shu pork!" he yells.

Right. Like I'd ever do that in the first place!

Chapter 33

THURSDAY MORNING

"LET ME GET this straight," Meg Worthington says. "You're trying to fix me up with your husband?"

"Yes."

"Your *current* husband."

"Yes."

"Because?"

"Ben's a great guy, and he deserves a great woman."

"But *you* don't want him."

"I didn't say *that*."

"Wait—are you trying to set up a *threesome?*"

"No, of *course* not!"

"You're what, trying to dump him gracefully?"

"Sort of. It's complicated."

Meg eyes me closely. "Does he still love you?"

"Yes."

"Doesn't sound complicated to *me*. Would you like to know what *I'm* hearing you say?"

People who talk like that tend to have some couch experience.

"Yes," I say.

"I'm hearing you say Ben's not good enough for *you*, so you've been looking around and decided that out of all the single women you know, Meg Worthington must be the most desperate."

"*What?*"

"So desperate is Meg Worthington, she'd *jump* at the chance of dating a married man who's still in love with his wife!"

"No, that's not it!"

"You said your husband deserves a great woman."

"He does!"

"And you've selected me?"

"Yes."

"Have we ever spoken?"

"Of *course!*"

"Beyond discussions about yoga?"

"Well..."

"Don't wrinkle your pretty little face worrying about it. The answer is we *haven't*. So you don't know if I'm a great woman or not."

"Well, you *seem* really nice. I mean, you're always pleasant..."

"That's about to change."

"I didn't mean to offend you, Meg. I honestly thought I'd be doing you both a favor."

She looks at me with amazement. "How did you expect this to work, Dani? Was I supposed to flirt with him, try to get him to go out with me? See if I could talk him into cheating on his wife?"

"Yes. I mean, he's available Monday and Tuesday evenings. I thought maybe I could prep you about him, and you could sort of bump into him and—"

"You're insane!" she says.

I watch her walk down the hall, heading toward the gym exit. But as she passes the snack bar she sees two friends and quickly pulls them into a gossip huddle. She's animated, they're stupefied. Now her friends are staring at me in horror. Sophie was right. This plan to find a woman for Ben isn't going to work.

My cell phone rings. Caller ID shows Patrick Aub.

"Hi Pat."

"Your boy came through."

I'm so off my game it takes me a few seconds. "*SeanInPain?*"

"That's the one."

"But I only told you about him yesterday!"

"Believe it or not, the kid's got a merchant account. Cheryl authorized payment for the shower pix, he sent her the download link."

I take a deep breath. "And?"

"The quality's outstanding."

"Pat?"

"Yeah?"

"Did you mean to say that?"

He laughs. "I forgot you didn't know."

I frown. I still don't know. I turn my back to Meg and her friends so I can use a more confidential tone on the phone.

Pat says, "Hold on, I'll forward you one."

"Wait. Are we breaking the law here? This is underage porn, right?"

I hear a gasp behind me and realize someone heard what I just said. I turn and see Meg standing there bug-eyed, with her mouth gaping open. Apparently she has something else to say, though I doubt she's changed her mind about dating Ben. I hold up my index finger and whisper, "Just a sec, Meg."

Pat says, "I just sent you the picture. Who's Meg? One of your hot friends?"

I turn away from Meg and whisper, "Is it legal?"

Pat says, "The law's currently fuzzy on this."

For a second I forget about Meg and say, "How can it be fuzzy if she's underage?"

"OMIGOD!" Meg shouts, and storms off. "OMIGOD!" she shouts as she walks past the snack bar. "OMIGOD!" as she exits the building.

I wonder how my comments about the law could have had such a major affect on her, so I play them back in my mind, and realize she only heard my side of the conversation, including:

This is underage porn, right? Is it legal? How can it be fuzzy if she's underage?

I have to face the facts. I have no right to lecture Dillon. Communication isn't my strong suit, either.

Pat says, "Let me know when it comes through."

Within seconds my phone shows I've got a download available. I click it and see *SeanInPain's* naked sister in the shower. Pat's right, the quality is outstanding.

But what I'm looking at is not a photograph. It's a beautiful full-color, cartoon-type drawing.

I click back to Pat. "I don't understand. What type of drawing is this?"

"It's called anime."

"Well, whatever it is, it's depicting an underage girl taking a shower."

"Like I say, the law's fuzzy on this issue."

"Who says?"

"Cheryl Goodman."

"Cheryl works in sex crimes?"

"Believe it or not, we have an Internet Crimes against Children unit. Cheryl says they're trying to establish laws against pornographic anime depicting minors. But as you can see, some of these perverts are highly-skilled artists, and they're demanding First Amendment rights."

"Does *Sean* even have a sister?"

"We don't know yet, but Cheryl doubts it. Her best guess is *Sean's* a middle-aged woman, and her internet rap about being a teen with an underage sister's a marketing ploy."

"*Sean's* a *woman?* That's quite a leap Cheryl's made."

"A woman who happens to be a highly-skilled artist. Look at the picture again."

I do.

"What about it?"

"According to our police sketch artist, the cutie-pie style suggests a female hand."

"That sounds sexist."

"Our sketch artist *is* a woman."

"Oh."

Pat gives me a quiet moment to think about it. Then I say, "But what about the degenerates who *buy* these pictures?"

"What about them?"

"Aren't they furious when they receive cartoons instead of photographs?"

"Apparently, they know what they're getting, because they've dealt with *Sean* in the past. The whole thing about helping him obtain the date rape drug, telling *Sean* what to do to his sister, is audience participation. They're helping *Sean* decide what types of pictures to draw."

"This is insane."

"It is. But the internet proves there's a market for every perversion. And men who are afraid to possess photos of actual children are willing to settle for cute cartoon drawings of children in sexual situations. In the end, whether guys are rubbing one out over porn stars or cartoons, it's all fantasy, right?"

"I wouldn't know."

He laughs.

"It's still pornography, Pat."

"I agree. But I'll ask you what Cheryl asked me an hour ago."

"What's that?"

"Have you ever seen paintings of naked babies in museums?"

"Of course."

"Should you be arrested for that?" He pauses, then says, "So where do you draw the line?"

"Sex acts?"

He chuckles. "You're a smart one, Dani. Don't let anyone tell you different."

"I already don't."

He chuckles again. Then says, "According to Cheryl, the government wants to make it a crime to draw, view, or possess drawings that depict underage children in sexual situations. Even cute cartoon figures."

"So this shower picture would be legal."

"For now. Technically. Probably. Like I say, it's fuzzy. This isn't the type of picture to build a case around."

"But *Sean's* next series? Cartoon drawings that depict him doing sexual things to his drugged, naked, underage sister?"

"That's the type they could take to court."

"So I've helped?"

"You've helped."

"What happens next?"

"For us? Nothing. It's not our jurisdiction."

"What do you mean?"

"*Sean* lives in Sacramento."

"But if Cheryl buys the next set and *Sean* mails them to her—"

"*Sean* doesn't mail. The photos are downloaded."

"But still—the purchase is *made* here in town. The pictures are *received* here in town."

"Doesn't matter. The crime, if there *is* one, took place where he offered the pictures for sale. We think."

"What you're saying, the police don't really know what to think."

"Not yet. This internet's a whole new ballgame. The laws haven't caught up yet. The good is really good, but the bad is still evolving. At any rate, Cheryl's going to pass along the info about *Sean* to the Sacramento PD. Maybe they'll look into it, maybe they won't."

Pat says I've helped, but I feel thoroughly defeated. And annoyed with myself for allowing this whole *Sean* thing to get me sidetracked. My mission is finding *ManChild*, not saving *Sean's* sister. I'd do well to remember that.

"Thanks, Pat."

"No sweat, kid. And remember, the offer's still on the table."

"The one about how if Ben and I have children you want to babysit?"

He laughs a good, hearty laugh. When it dies down he says, "Try again."

"The one about if Ben and I break up, you want to be my boyfriend?"

"That's the one."

Chapter 34

"I GIVE UP, Sofe. I'm done with it."

"No. You're just beaten down. Step away for a couple of days. Or weeks."

"When I think of the hundreds of hours I've wasted..."

"You haven't wasted those hours. You'll catch the bastard someday."

I'm at my office, on the phone. I told Sophie about *SeanInPain*, and how frustrated I am that the whole internet thing is yielding no results. I'm feeling defeated.

"I don't know," I say. "What if all these chat rooms turn out to be marketing people selling cartoon pornography?"

"You're doing this for Jaqui Moreland."

I sigh. "Good point."

"Look, you just need some TLC. You're still planning to come on Sunday?"

"I wouldn't miss it for the world."

"Good. I know you're feeling down right now, but we're going to have a great time, I promise."

"I believe you."

"I'm so excited, Dani! I've got you for three full days!"

"Maybe you'll get bored with me."

Sophie pauses. "What else happened?"

I say nothing.

"Spill, girl. This isn't about *SeanInPain*. I've never heard you sound so down. Seriously, what's happened?"

I start crying.

Then I tell her about Roy's visit yesterday, and how he threatened to expose my identity.

"He would never do that," she says.

"You don't know him. He's pond scum. He'd do it for the worst reason in the world."

"What's that?"

"Because he can."

"Is that your office phone ringing in the background?" she says.

"Yup. But I don't care."

"You need to answer it, Dani. Might be a real PI job!"

"I'd rather talk to you."

"Answer the phone, then call me back."

"Okay."

I pick up the phone on the fifth ring.

"Hello?"

It's Ben, and he's not in a good mood. At all. He says, "I just got an interesting call."

My heart sinks. Roy came through. The media has found me. Our lives are over.

"Do you want to hear about my call?" he asks.

"Where are you?"

"Home."

"Are you feeling any better?"

"No."

"Do you want me to come home? I can stop by the drugstore on my way."

"Stop being nice to me. Can't you tell I'm furious?"

"Did you lose your job?"

"No Dani, it's Thursday. I have two morning classes and two afternoon classes on Thursdays. You'd know this if you paid the slightest bit of attention to me. But since you don't, I should probably point out that when I'm between classes on Thursdays, I often come home for a couple of hours. Which is why I was here when the interesting call came in."

I say nothing, so Ben jumps right in with, "Do you know a Meg Worthington from yoga class?"

"Oh shit!"

"Meg informed me you tried to recruit her to have an affair with me this morning. She also said you're planning to divorce me."

"That's not true."

"Which part?"

I sigh. "Let's not do this now, over the phone."

"Why? Is there someone in your office?"

"No. It's just—"

"There's another guy, isn't there?"

"No. I promise there's not."

"Then what the hell's going on? Does the whole town know you're trying to fix me up?"

"No."

"Well, have you asked anyone else?"

"Um…"

"I don't believe this. What's going on, Dani? Seriously, what is it you want?"

I take a deep breath. "I think maybe it's time we should start dating other women."

"*Excuse me?*"

"I mean, *you*! I think it's time *you* should start dating other women. We're not happy together, Ben. I want you to find someone who makes you happy."

He pauses before saying, "You make me happy, Dani. Only you."

"Well, maybe *I'm* not all that happy."

He pauses again. "I gave you the two days a week to do whatever it is you're doing. I sleep alone. We have sex twice a year."

"Like I said, you're not happy."

He hangs up.

I hang up.

Then the phone rings again.

"Ben," I say, "Seriously, let's—"

The voice on the other end cuts me off. It isn't Ben. It's a reporter from one of the local TV stations. She asks if it's true.

"Is what true?"

"Are you really Mindy Renee Whittaker?"

Chapter 35

I SLAM THE phone down, grab my handbag and my laptop, and race out the door. With keys in hand, I run to my car, looking side to side for the media mob.

So far so good!

If I can get out of here before the throng of traffic blocks my exit, I might be able to escape.

You probably think I'm awfully full of myself, or that I'm being overly dramatic. Or maybe you think I have an overinflated ego regarding my newsworthiness.

But this isn't my first rodeo.

You've seen people on the news, walking with their attorneys to or from a courthouse, surrounded by dozens of reporters, yelling, barking out questions. Looks like a busy crowd, doesn't it? But the footage you've seen on TV was probably shot at close range. If the cameras were to pan a wider area, you'd see people and cars moving along in the background, completely oblivious to the activity being filmed.

That wasn't the case when I walked out of the police station after my encounter with Collin Tyler Hicks. On that occasion the downtown streets of Portland had been blocked off, and thousands of reporters, photographers, and well-wishers were so tightly packed, you couldn't have wedged a sheet of paper between them. Thousands upon thousands of people were pushing and shouting at the same time, all wanting a piece of me. It was...

It was overwhelming.

And this story will be just as big:

Here she is, folks, the little girl who got away. The one you didn't see on a TV movie of the week, because she and her mother never authorized the story. And now she's all grown up. Sadly, her mother died four years ago, during an operation, so she's an orphan this time around! But she's also a wife, living quietly among us! What's her story? Where does she live? Does she have kids? A job? What does she eat?

I gun the gas pedal and roar out of the parking lot, into the street. Each red light is agony, but eventually I'm on the expressway, where I remind myself to relax. I take a deep breath, safe for now.

I use the hands-free phone feature in my car to call Sophie.

"Who called you at the office?" she says.

"Two people. First Ben, then a TV reporter."

"Oh shit."

"That's what I said when Ben told me Meg Worthington called him."

"What? Who's that?"

"The latest and last of the *Date My Husband* contestants."

"Did you say the last?"

"Yup. I've come to my senses. Ben will have to find his own dates from now on."

She laughs. Then says, "What did the reporter want?"

"She wanted to know if I'm Mindy Renee Whittaker."

"That fucking Roy!" Sophie says. "I could *kill* him!"

"What are you going to do, call Uncle Sal from the deli?"

"Say the word and I will."

I laugh. "Roy's a douche. If it wasn't him, it'd be someone else. It had to happen sooner or later. It was just a matter of time."

"Uh, Dani?"

"Yeah?"

"How come you sound so calm?"

"What do you mean?"

"Last few times we spoke you were either crying or about to cry. Right now, when you should be sobbing, you're cool as a cucumber."

I think about it. "You're right. I'm energized. My life is over and I'm sort of...happy about it."

"Maybe the lemon is finally ready to come out of the bottle."

"Orange."

"Whatever."

"Maybe you're right," I say.

"Where are you now?"

"In my car."

"Are you headed home? You *can't* go home, it'll be a circus."

"According to the last sign, I'm on my way to Nashville."

"You're kidding!"

"Don't worry, I won't lead the media to you."

"Nonsense. You'll come straight here and park in my garage. This is a perfect place to hide."

"They'll find me, eventually."

"Yes. But in the meantime we can strategize."

"I'm still four hours away. You've got plenty of time to change your mind."

"Why would I change my mind? I *want* you here."

"If the media finds out, you could lose your career."

"What's there to find out, Dani?"

"You know."

"That we're friends?"

"They might think it's more than that."

"I'd be honored if they do."

"You might want to re-think that."

"Why?"

"You're a country singer/songwriter. Your fans are conservative. They have no idea you consider yourself gay, and of course, I live with you two nights a week. Not to mention I'm married! Stop me if any of these revelations sound like career boosters!"

"Dani, listen to yourself."

"What do you mean?"

"You sound *fantastic*! I think you're secretly very excited."

"You're crazy."

"See you in four, sugar pants."

"What? *Excuse me*? What did you just call me?"

Sophie laughs and hangs up.

I laugh too, then wonder why. When I think about it, I realize Sophie's right about my mood. I can't deny I'm feeling a certain adrenalin rush. I feel alive, and oddly enough, a strange sense of freedom. It suddenly dawns on me that instead of ruining my life, this announcement might simply change it.

Chapter 36

OVER THE NEXT four hours Ben calls me fifteen times, trying to track me down. His voice messages have grown increasingly frantic. Here's the most recent one:

Dani, please pick up! It's a circus here! Reporters are camped all over the yard and down the street. I'm a prisoner in my own home! And I don't feel well. Like I'm coming down with the flu, or something. Where are you?

I'd answer his calls, but what he really wants to know is where I am. And that's something I don't care to explain right now.

Sophie calls.

"Dani, oh my God, you're all over the news!"

"Ben says they're camped out at the house."

"You spoke to him?"

"No. But he's left a dozen messages."

"They're showing live footage of your office *and* your house. They're interviewing your neighbors! They're showing your *baby* pictures—you were really cute, by the way—and your grade school and junior high pictures."

"Not the one where my two front teeth are missing!"

"That's the one!"

"Please tell me you're kidding."

"Oh, hush. It's adorable."

"I don't believe this!"

Ugh.

"Let's talk about your neighbors," I say.

"What about them?"

"I've been staying with you two nights a week for months. Someone's bound to turn me in."

"They're not thinking Nashville, so it won't cross anyone's mind."

"It might from here on out."

"True. Call just before entering the neighborhood and I'll open my garage. You can pull right in and I'll shut the door behind you."

"I should disguise myself. You don't by any chance happen to have a wig, do you?"

"I'm a country singer, remember?"

"Where do you keep them? I've never seen any wigs at your place."

"I just have two, and one's blonde, so that's no good. I keep them in a dresser drawer. You've never gone through my drawers when I was out?"

"Of course not! Have you gone through mine?"

"Are you kidding? Of course I have! Every square inch!"

"You're terrible!"

"But thorough."

"What's happening now?"

"Hang on, I'll turn up the volume."

I hear her TV in the background, but can't understand what's being said, so I keep driving till Sophie says, "They're interviewing people at the gym where you work out."

"I don't know any of the afternoon people."

"Maybe not, but they've all got something to say about you!"

"What's the verdict?"

"You're quiet. You don't cause any trouble. You seem nice enough, but some find it odd you won't shower there. Now a psychologist is explaining you probably have some deep-seated issues that preclude you from getting naked in front of others."

"Maybe they'll interview Carter Teague or Roy and hear a different story."

Sophie laughs, then says, "Where are you now?"

"East of E-town. Thanks for letting me stay, Sofe. You're a good friend. I hope I don't create problems for you."

"We'll get you through this, Dani."

Chapter 37

BY THE TIME I arrive, Sophie's got the coffee brewed, the TV on, and a blanket on the sofa. First thing I do is try on her wig.

"It's auburn," I say.

"It's perfect," she says.

I get to the nearest mirror and start laughing.

"I look ridiculous!"

"You look incredible!"

We sip coffee and talk and soon it feels like old times. I tell her the things Roy said in my office. When I get to the part where he claimed Ben had a thing for me at age fifteen, she raises an eyebrow, but says nothing. I go all in and tell her about sleeping with Ben Tuesday night.

"You really sniffed my perfume while doing it?"

"I really did."

"Dani, it's time for me to break the news to you."

"What news?'"

"You're officially gay!"

"You think?"

"I'd love the chance to find out!"

"If we do, I'll put Ben's cologne on my hand first."

She calls me a shithead and we laugh hysterically.

Why?

Because there's a lot of estrogen in the room and we're together. And Sophie feels needed, and I feel safe.

It's a good combination.

Sophie says, "All jokes aside, I'd know in a heartbeat if you brought a different scent into the bedroom."

"I'd know, too. So why not Ben?"

"Why do you think? He's a man."

Speaking of Ben, I feel bad about not checking in with him, especially if he's picked up a flu bug. But I'm afraid to call the house in case the phone's been tapped. I'm also concerned they might have cell phone monitoring devices that could pick up our conversation. I'd hate for the whole world to hear us talking about Meg Worthington, or about how great the sex was for Ben on Tuesday night!

"Since you're already paranoid," Sophie says, "you might want to remove the battery from your cell phone. That way they can't pinpoint your location."

"Good point," I say.

I text Ben to let him know I'm safe and in hiding, and tell him I hope he feels better soon. I tell him not to worry about me, and end with the numbers 143, which means, I Love You.

As soon as the text is sent, I remove my battery.

"I've just gone dark, Thelma!" I tell Sophie.

"You're on the lam, Louise!" she responds.

We make popcorn and channel surf into the night as one station after another rolls out the old photos of Colin Tyler Hicks, and the basement where he kept me, and the footage of my bruised and battered face when I walked into the precinct house. Each station trots out behavioral experts and psychiatrists and asks their own version of the question, *Where is Dani Ripper, a.k.a. Mindy Renee Whittaker, and what's going on in her head right now?*

"And why does anyone *care?*" I say to the TV.

Chapter 38

FRIDAY MORNING

I WAKE TO the scent of freshly-roasted coffee and wonder if I'm dreaming. Then remember where I am, and what happened yesterday. I take a quick shower, towel-dry my hair, wrap myself in a white, terrycloth robe and pad downstairs.

"Hey, sleepyhead," Sophie says. "I'm so glad you were able to sleep in."

I yawn and look at the clock.

7:15 a.m. And I'm already showered.

"You call this sleeping in?"

"For you? Today? Yeah, Dani!"

She points to the morning paper on the counter.

"Already?" I say.

"Front page."

I hold out a mug, Sophie fills it.

"And on TV?"

She shakes her head. "You don't want to know."

I smile. "How bad can it be?"

"They found out you've been trying to find *ManChild*."

I do a double-take. You may not believe this, given my reaction to recent events, but I'm probably the least moody or bad-tempered person you know. But this announcement takes me from zero to furious in one second flat. I feel the red creeping into my cheeks. This is as pissed as I get. I'm so angry I can't speak.

"I'm sorry, Dani," Sophie says. "I wish it weren't true."

"Do they have any idea what they've *done?*" I shout. "Now he'll *never* get caught!"

She brings some fresh cut pineapple to the table, and a little box of toothpicks. I'm still furious, but the scent of her coffee is heavenly, and I do love my fresh pineapple in the morning. She sits quietly till I sip some coffee.

"It's good, Sofe."

She reaches across the small wooden table that cost tons of money to craft into what appears to be an authentic early American antique, and puts her hand on mine.

I put my other hand over hers and look into her eyes and say, "Now he knows I'm after him. He'll be on his guard. He's going to kill more children."

"Actually, on TV they're saying just the opposite."

"What do you mean?"

"People love you, Dani. You have no idea how much! They said more than a dozen private detectives from all over the country have already called in to radio and TV stations to offer their services, free of charge. They want to find the bastard and put him away as a favor to you. They're challenging PI's all over the country to pitch in and help you get this guy."

"People *love* me? What are you talking about? They don't love me. They just want to hear the details about what Colin Tyler Hicks and I did to each other in that basement."

"Honey," she says, "nine years ago it was about the crime. This time it's about you."

"I have no idea what that means."

"Last time you were their victim. This time you're their hero."

"I don't want to be a hero, Sofe, I just want a normal life and a chance to catch *ManChild*."

"Dani, this could be huge! Not twenty minutes ago *The Today Show* said, and I quote, 'Dani Ripper, the little girl who got away, is once again the most famous face in America.'"

"How do they know what I look like?"

"They're posting pictures."

"Recent photos?"

"Yup."

"Where did they get them?"

"From your business manager."

"My *what*? I don't have a business manager! Who's making *that* claim?"

"The vodka bottle."

"The...*Ben?*"

"Yes. The Ben."

Chapter 39

"BEN WOULDN'T DO that!"

Sophie gives me a look that embodies all the things I love about her. In the space of a few seconds I see sadness, sympathy, compassion, and best of all, understanding—in her face and eyes. Then she says, "I'm sorry, Dani. But Ben's trying to cash in."

I stare off into space a full minute before turning back to her. When I do, I fix my eyes on hers and say, "You're insulting my husband. And when you do that, you're insulting me."

She nods.

Without taking my eyes off hers I say, "I think you owe me an apology."

She bites her lip.

"Ben would never, *ever* do that," I say.

She holds my gaze, but doesn't apologize.

As the tears well in my eyes, I stand and say, "I'm going to remove all my things from your house now."

I start walking out of the kitchen, but Sophie says something that stops me in my tracks.

"Ben made a public announcement this morning."

I turn back to face her. "If you want us to remain friends, tell me only what you know to be true. If Ben were talking about you, I'd make him do the same."

She gets to her feet and walks toward me, but stops when we're three feet apart. Her cheeks are streaked with tears.

I say, "You're crying worse than I am."

"That's because I love you more. It's moments like these when I realize just how much I adore you. You're the most loyal person in the world. It warms my heart to see you standing up for Ben like this, even as it crushes me to tell you what he's done."

"What's he done?"

"He announced he's accepting bids from publishers for his book."

"What book?"

"*Mindy and Me*. The true story of what happened to Mindy Renee Whittaker."

Chapter 40

"WHAT HAPPENED?" I say.

I'm on the floor in Sophie's hallway, with a pillow under my head. She's lying beside me. I notice a pillow under her head, too. There's also a blanket over us.

"You passed out," she says. "I tried to catch you, but you took me down with you. You woke up instantly, and said you wanted to stay on the floor. So I got up, got the pillows and blanket."

"Why the blanket?"

She pauses.

I look at her.

"You're blushing," I say.

"Well...you only had the robe on, and..."

I lift the blanket high enough to peek under it.

"How much did you see?"

"Not everything."

"No?"

"Your shoulders and arms were covered."

"Ah."

"You don't seem to remember the whole pillows and blanket thing," Sophie says. "Are you okay?"

"I think so. How long have I been lying here?"

"You don't know? I mean, we've been *talking* to each other."

My expression tells her I don't have a clue.

"We've been like this for nearly an hour. You've been crying, and staring into space. I've talked to you, stroked your hair, and you kept telling me to let you lie here."

We lie silently a few more minutes. Then I say, "I suppose you have proof about Ben writing the book?"

"I saw the interview where he said it. I'm sure we can find it on the internet."

"Sofe?"

"Yeah honey?"

"Help me up?"

"I'd be glad to."

She does.

"Are you dizzy?"

"Not at all. Why, did I hit my head?"

"No. You sort of fell on me."

"Did you hit *your* head?"

She smiles, takes my left hand in hers, and places it on the back of her head so I can feel the lump.

"Sofe! I'm so sorry! You're okay?"

"I'm fine."

We're a foot apart, eyes locked. Mine are blue, hers, brown. I'm blonde, she's brunette. Our heights are so closely matched you'd need a carpenter's level to see who's taller. But I'm high-waisted, so my legs are slightly longer. We're both petite. She's got boobs and hips, I'm more athletic in shape. I'm twenty-four, she's twenty-nine.

In other words, we're identical. And perfect together.

I keep my left hand on the back of her head, and touch the palm of my right hand to her cheek. And there, in the hallway between Sophie Alexander's kitchen and den, at precisely 8:18 a.m. on the morning my world has imploded, I close my eyes and kiss my best friend full on the lips, hear her joyful murmur, accept her tongue, share mine, and finally, pull away.

"Holy *shit!*" Sophie says, moving in for another.

I hold her away with a reluctant hand. Then give her a quick kiss and say, "I'm still married, Sofe."

"As married as you are straight?"

"Probably."

"And I suppose you'll want to check your computer about Ben's book."

"Yes."

She sighs. "Want to take some pineapple upstairs with you?"

"Depends on what *you're* going to do."

"If I were a guy I'd take a cold shower! Since I'm not, I plan to get comfy in the den, turn on the TV, and watch for breaking news about my best friend."

"Can I bring my laptop down and surf the net while we watch TV together?"

"Are you going to wear your silly pajamas?"

"Can I?"

"I'd be disappointed if you didn't."

"In that case, I'll see you in five minutes. In the den."

Chapter 41

SOPHIE WASN'T LYING about Ben. Three of the Big Six publishers are considering entering a bidding war for his book, provided I give my blessing. Ben says he found time to write every Monday and Tuesday for nearly a year, and only recently completed his journal. He claims he never intended to turn it into a book, but when the news about my identity broke, he thought, "Why not?"

I check several online sources and find similar content. Ben's credentials are mentioned, and he explains he's been my teacher, my confessor, and my lover, and claims to have practically raised me these past six years. Those claims are generally true. Not to mention he helped me cope with the loss of my mother after she died on the operating table at City Hospital four years ago.

Sophie interrupts me from time to time, with, "Dani! Check it out!" or "Did you hear *that?*" But it's mostly a rehashing of old news. I'm pleased and gratified to see the list of private eyes who've signed the pledge to bring down *ManChild* has grown to twenty. They're calling themselves *Dani's Detectives!*

As I lazily review yet another article about how Ben Davis's book deal is expected to fetch between one and two million dollars, I click the link on his name and it takes me to his biographical data. Where he grew up, where he went to high school and college. There's a link on the word college, and it takes me to a website where Gator alumni can view their former classmates. I glance at the TV and see a commercial featuring a famous quarterback throwing passes in a backyard pickup game, talking about the jeans he wears. The commercial reminds me of Roy's football story, so whatever it is that makes private investigators think the way we do—causes me to click on Gator Football, which eventually takes me to their football schedule for Roy's junior year.

I must've made a noise because Sophie says, "What's up?"

"They didn't play Georgia Tech."

I type some more, and Sophie comes over to sit beside me.

"I didn't catch that," she says.

"Ben and Roy went to University of Florida."

"So?"

"Roy said because of Ben's prank he missed the Georgia Tech game, and had to sit on the bench when the team played in the Independence Bowl."

"But they didn't play Georgia Tech?"

"Right."

"Maybe it was their sophomore year."

"Florida didn't play Georgia Tech the entire decade."

"You checked all that just now?"

"There's a chart that shows the Gator football schedule since the beginning of time. And guess how many times Florida has played in the Independence Bowl throughout history?"

"I have no idea."

"Never!"

She studies my face. "I know this is big news, but I'm not sure why. What you're saying, Roy lied about the football games. Why's that such a big deal?"

"It means he lied about why he had a grudge against Ben all these years."

"So it must've been some other reason?"

"Or none at all."

Sophie frowns. "You lost me."

"Until last week, Ben has never mentioned Roy. Not once. If he had, I'd remember. Now, according to both of them, they've maintained regular correspondence every year."

"So what are you thinking?"

"What if Ben set me up instead of Roy?"

Chapter 42

SOPHIE'S EYES GROW big. "But...*how?*"

"I'm just walking through this, seeing how it sounds out loud," I say.

"I *love* it when you talk PI," she says. "Please, go on!"

"When Ben and I came to our understanding about me sleeping upstairs and being gone two days a week, he figured it was just a matter of time before I left him. So he decided to write a book that would make him a millionaire. He accommodated my crazy demands so I'd stay with him."

"Why? He already knew your story."

"Ben knew the world had to see us as a happily married couple. Otherwise, they'd label it a revenge book."

"And that would be a problem because?"

"A tell-all book, written by a bitter ex-husband, would be denounced by the media. But a book written with my help and consent would be welcomed with open arms."

Sophie says, "I see where this is going. But I want to hear you do the lead in."

"If I'm Ben and I've written a million-dollar story that can't be published because I have to protect my dear wife's identity, what's the best thing that can possibly happen?"

Sophie raises her hand, pretending to be an eager student in school. "Ooh! I know! I know! Call on me!" she says.

She's excited. Her face, animated.

I remember our kiss.

"You're into role play?" I say.

"Of *course*! But if we play *teacher's pet*, I get to be teacher."

I stare at her blankly.

To my complete shock, Sophie goes into character. "Dani?" Then she uses a small girl's voice to represent me. "*Yes, Miss Alexander?*" —"You've been naughty, Dani. Very, very naughty. You'll have to stay after school and help me with some chores." —"*Yes, Miss Alexander.*"

She winks at me, and I shake my head, wondering what the hell I've gotten myself into. This is a side of Sophie I've never seen. I stare at her incredulously as she keeps the fantasy going.

"Dani?" —"*Yes, Miss Alexander?* —"Climb up the ladder and fetch me the blue book on the top shelf. Don't worry, I'll hold the ladder for you." —"*But Miss Alexander, I'm wearing a skirt! You'll be able to see my pretty pink panties!*" —"It's okay, Dani. I'm your teacher. Now hurry up, there are lots of books to fetch from the shelf."

I roll my eyes.

She says "Whew!" and pats her heart, as if breathless, and gives me another wink. "What do you think?"

I frown. "You screwed up my big aha moment."

"What? Oh. Sorry. But we both know what you've done."

"Which is?"

"You've cracked the case."

"You see it, yes?"

"Of course,' Sophie says. "Ben got Roy to set you up."

"Because?"

"He couldn't personally reveal your identity. The media would crucify him."

"Exactly," I say, "and his book is ready to go at the exact moment in history the world wants to read it!"

"And Ben gets to do media interviews and talk shows!"

"But there's one thing that doesn't add up," I say.

"What's that?"

"All Ben needed Roy to do is blow my cover. Why go through the whole thing with Carter Teague?"

"To take nude photos of you?"

I pause a minute before saying, "You know what I think?"

"What?"

"I think Roy concocted that scheme on his own."

"Why?"

"Ben doesn't have any money, so he probably asked Roy to break the news to the media as a favor. Roy probably checked around and learned I've done some decoy work. He and Carter are either married or dating, and Roy got her to set me up so they could take the photos of me."

"To blackmail you?" Sophie says.

"To blackmail Ben, and make him share the book royalties."

"Or sell the pictures on the internet."

I think about that, and remember how Carter kept trying to talk me into leaving the door open between our hotel rooms. At the time I was worried she might be planning to video me, and now I think my initial instinct was right. When I locked the connecting door she was forced to use her cell phone camera as a backup.

Sophie says, "Roy could break the news about you being Mindy Renee, then cash in on your world-wide popularity by selling, or threatening to sell your nude photos."

"Right. But I nipped that in the bud by destroying the pictures at the restaurant."

I stare into space a minute, thinking.

"What?" Sophie says.

"Wednesday, in my office, Roy asked if I wanted to know what I could do to keep him from going public with the news. And I said I didn't want to hear it."

"What do you think he was talking about?"

"Letting him take more nude photos."

"So he could get back in the game," she says. "But he broke the news anyway."

"Probably got a nice chunk of change from the tabloids."

"What a jerk," Sophie says.

"He certainly is."

"Actually, I was talking about Ben," she says. If you're right about how all this happened, Ben's a bigger jerk than Roy."

"We don't have proof that Ben had anything to do with it," I remind her. "And all that talk about how Ben had a weird thing for me when I was fifteen? We've only got Roy's word for any of that being true. And think about this: if Roy's telling the truth, it would have to be the biggest coincidence in history."

"What coincidence?"

"That Ben fell in love with me when I was fifteen, living in Portland, and two years later he somehow tracked my mom and me down and got a tutoring job?" That's ridiculous. What happened, Ben was out of work and posted he was a former college professor looking for tutoring jobs. He didn't find us, my mom found *him*."

"I don't care about that part," she says. "I'm convinced Ben is guilty. One hundred percent."

I look at her curiously. "Are you just saying that because you want to get into my pretty pink panties?"

"Yes, absolutely!" she says, smiling.

"You know my answer to that."

"You're still married?"

"Yup."

She sighs. "Such a pity."

Chapter 43

"I'VE GOT BOMBSHELL news!" I announce, thirty minutes later.

Sophie comes running in from the kitchen.

"Spill!" she says.

I point to my computer screen. "Want to see what Roy looks like?"

She jumps onto the couch and moves as close to me as she can get.

"That's him in college?"

"It is. But you know what?"

"What?"

"This isn't the Roy I met."

"Well, he's probably changed. I mean, it's been how many years?"

"Doesn't matter."

She cocks her head and gives me a curious look. "Why not?"

"Ben's college roommate, the real Roy Burroughs, died in a car crash ten years ago."

Sophie grins. "The plot thickens!"

I give her a look. "How long have you been waiting to say that?"

"Since the day we met, and you told me you were a private eye."

I laugh.

Sophie says, "So this proves I'm right? About Ben being the biggest jerk in the world?"

"It does. Ben found someone to play Roy, and fabricated the whole college story so I wouldn't be suspicious."

"Do you think the fake Roy was hoping to blackmail Ben?"

"Either that, or Ben intended to use the photos as insurance."

"Insurance for what?"

"To make sure I gave him permission to sell the book. Of course, that would mean Ben knew I was doing decoy work. And I find that hard to believe, since it never came up."

"You know what I think?" Sophie says.

"It's time to call Ben?"

"Exactly."

I put the battery back in the phone and press a button. Sophie says, "I can't believe he's number one on your speed dial instead of me."

"Oh, stop!" I say, laughing.

Ben answers with "Where the hell *are* you? I'm sick as a *dog!*"

"You didn't look sick on TV, talking about your *book.*"

"Well. About that—"

I interrupt with, "How's Roy?"

He skips a beat before responding. "What are you *talking* about?"

"Roy, your college roommate."

"What about him?"

"I was surprised to learn he's been *dead* for ten years."

Ben goes silent a minute. Then says, "What else do you know?"

"I know you set me up with him and Carter Teague."

"How the hell do you know Carter? And what do you mean, set you up?"

My turn to pause. "Carter Teague? The woman Roy hired?"

"I don't know what you're talking about. Hired for what?"

"Never mind." I cover the phone and whisper, "The decoy job was Roy's idea." To Ben I say, "Let's talk about your book."

"What about it?"

"You can't publish without my consent. It's my story."

"We're married. You'll get half the proceeds. For doing absolutely *nothing* by the way."

"You planned this whole thing. You lived with me all this time, knowing you were going to sell me out."

"Give me a break, Dani. You lived with me all this time knowing you were going to leave me. You tried to talk other women into having an affair with me! And I had to give you two nights a week outside the marriage, no questions asked? Are you *insane?* Of *course* I wanted to benefit from this stupid, one-sided marriage."

"I'll admit I've been a rotten wife for more than a year. But I wouldn't have called our marriage stupid."

He sighs. "I'm not without guilt in our marriage."

"What do you mean?"

"I married you, knowing you didn't love me."

"I loved you back then."

"I doubt that's true, though I certainly loved you enough for both of us. But I took advantage of your confusion. I was selfish."

"Where'd you find Roy?"

"He's a drama professor at Riverton."

Riverton College was Ben's employer before we met. They fired him when Erica's affair became a *YouTube* sensation.

"I thought you didn't have friends at Riverton," I say.

"He's not a friend. But he owed me a huge favor. And he's a good actor, don't you think?"

"What's the huge favor you did for him?"

"He was sleeping with the dean's wife."

"So?"

"I knew, but kept it quiet."

"Why's that such a big favor?"

"I saved his job. And it was a very hard secret for me to keep."

"Why?"

"This is the same dean who fired me because my wife became famous for cheating on me. It would've been fun to tell him his wife was cheating on him."

"How much did you pay this drama professor?"

"I gave him my life's savings. Eight thousand dollars. As a guarantee."

"Against what the tabloids were willing to pay?"

"That's right. I gambled my entire future on this book."

"And you're willing to sell me out, and turn my life into a media circus?"

"Only because I thought—and still think—it could bring us together again."

"But if not, you're willing to cash in."

"Dani? My heart has always been in the right place where you're concerned. *You're* the one making plans to leave. But yes, faced with a life without you, it would be nice to have something positive in my life to fall back on."

"I want to read the manuscript before you sign a contract."

"I can arrange that."

He pauses, then says, "Are you coming home?"

"Email the manuscript to me."

"It's on the way. Are you?"

"Not today."

"Soon?"

"I don't know."

Chapter 44

"YOU STARTED STRONG, but ended meek," Sophie says. "What happened in the middle?"

"He made me feel sorry for him."

She shakes her head. "You're a helluva good person."

"If I were a good person, none of this would've happened."

"I won't even bother to dissect that comment. Is he sending you his manuscript?"

I smile.

"What?"

"I like how you said that." I imitate her, saying, "I won't even bother to dissect that comment."

"I don't sound like that," she says. Then asks, "Can I read Ben's book?"

"Of course."

Moments later the manuscript shows up in an attachment. I download it and forward a copy to Sophie. She's in the recliner, I'm on the couch. We both have our laptops.

"Shall we?" I say.

"I'll race you!" she says.

We pause for lunch, a bathroom break, and order Chinese food for delivery. I note Sophie has known me only a year, but managed to order what I like—steamed rice and vegetables, with garlic sauce—without having to ask.

After dinner, unlike Ben, Sophie makes a big production out of opening our fortune cookies.

"Omigod!" she squeals, after reading hers. "Check this out!" She holds it up to my face. It reads, *You will find happiness with a close friend!*

We look at each other and smile.

"Well done, Sofe!"

"Read yours!" she says.

I do, and laugh.

"What?" she says.

I hand it to her. She reads it out loud. "*You will find happiness with a close friend!*

She says, "Omigod! What are the chances we'd both get the same one?"

I say, "There are two more cookies in the bag. What are the chances they'll say the same thing?"

"I don't want to know what they say. I'm happy with these."

I reach into the bag, open one of the others.

"Go ahead, Sophie says."

I read, "*Please send help! I'm being held prisoner in a Chinese bakery!*"

"That is such an old joke!" she says, and grabs the other one and pretends to read "*You will be hungry again in one hour!*"

"That is so lame!" I say.

We laugh and exchange the fortunes and learn that, sure enough, all four offer happiness with a close friend.

"You still think this was an error in packaging?" Sophie says.

"I know it was. But I like it."

"We're going to have to work on this, you and me."

"Work on what?"

"The fact you're not romantic."

"Not true," I say.

"I love you, Dani, but you're not *even* romantic."

"Am too!"

"Give me one example," Sophie says.

"I put your perfume on my hand."

"Well..."

"I wear silly pajamas because you like them."

"I thought *you* liked them!"

"I like them when I'm with you."

"Okay, that's romantic," she says.

"And there's more," I say.

Before she responds, I head for her garage. When I come back in, I'm carrying a small ladder. I set it up next to her bookcase and climb three steps.

Using my best school girl voice, I say, "Miss Alexander? I can't seem to find the blue book. What should I do?"

Sophie laughs.

I make a point to shake my butt while pretending to search for the book.

"Oh, my God," she says, laughing even harder. "Those pajamas!"

I look down at her. "Which is better, plaid skirt or silly pajamas?"

"Plaid skirt."

"Too bad I don't have one."

"I do," she says.

"Sofe," I say. "*Seriously?*"

She laughs. "I've got a closet full."

"A closet full?"

"Well, a section of my closet, if we're being technical."

"All school girl uniforms?"

"Of course not! What do you think, I'm weird or something?"

I laugh. Doing my best to imitate her voice, I say, "I won't even bother to dissect that comment."

She frowns. "That's twice. You really think I sound like that?"

"In my head? Yes, absolutely. But no matter who I'm imitating, what comes out my mouth always sounds like Meg, from Hercules."

"Great heroine," she says.

"Tough, classy lady," I agree. "Meg's my favorite cartoon character."

"Interesting," Sophie says, arching an eyebrow.

"What is?"

"In the movie, Meg was hired to seduce the powerful Hercules. In real life you've been hired to seduce powerful men. I wonder what a psychiatrist would make of that."

She's expecting me to make a defensive comment. For that reason alone, I decide not to say anything.

Sophie says, "So, do you want pleats or plain?"

I stare at her blankly.

"The school girl skirts," she says. "Pleated or plain?"

"Hold that thought," I say, climbing down the ladder. "We've still got some reading to do."

Sophie sighs. "Like I said, no sense of romance."

Chapter 45

WHEN WE'VE BOTH finished reading the manuscript I ask Sophie what she thinks.

"It's a snooze."

"Why?"

"Too clinical. It reads like a police report."

"I get that, too," I say. "You think it's because we know Ben's an educator, not a writer?"

"I think it's because he wasn't there, and it shows."

She pauses, then says, "You know what I think?"

"What's that?"

"I think you need to file an injunction against this book, and write your own."

"What? Write my own book? Are you crazy?"

"Why not?"

"Well, for one thing, I can barely spell. I've got a basic GED education, remember?"

"You're witty and clever. And one of the smartest people I know."

"That's because you're in show business."

"See what I mean? You're witty."

"I can't write a book. I wouldn't even know how to start."

"We'll hire a ghost writer."

"Hire? As in pay someone?"

"Why not? I'll call Charlie Yang, see what he says."

"Charlie Yang?"

"My agent. He'll know someone we can contact."

"No offense, Sofe, but I think my first contact should be an attorney, not a talent agent. Do you have an attorney?"

"Paul Small."

"Is he any good?"

"I wouldn't know the difference, but according to Charlie, he's the best."

Sophie calls Paul, and puts me on the phone. I tell him my story, and he agrees to represent me. When he tells me his rate is two hundred fifty an hour, I repeat it out loud in disbelief.

Sophie says, "I'll take care of the legal fees till your royalties come in."

She takes the phone and tells the attorney to bill her instead of me, and asks about filing an injunction against Ben's book. I don't hear what he says, but there's a lot of discussion back and forth.

"Ask if he can recommend a ghost writer," I say.

She does, and they talk about that. While doing so she pulls a paper towel from the rack and writes something on it with a felt-tip pen. After hanging up she says, "He wants to talk to someone in his office before advising you about the injunction."

"What did he say about a ghostwriter?"

"As it turns out, Paul's got a client who's an author."

"What's his name?"

"*Her* name is..."

She picks up the paper towel and squints to make out her handwriting. "Janie Ramirez."

"How does it work?"

"She interviews you, records the conversation, then writes the book. Her name won't even appear on the cover."

"Janie should get credit if she's doing the writing."

"She's getting paid to edit your transcript. But if it makes you feel better you can thank her in the Acknowledgements."

"What's that?"

She laughs.

"What?"

"You're hopeless."

"Do we call her?"

"Paul's calling her right now. He said she'll probably call us in a few minutes."

"This was your idea," I say.

"So?"

"When she calls, will *you* talk to her?"

"Sure. I'll tell her *my* story."

"What story is that?"

"The one where I have to drag my girlfriend kicking and screaming all the way to the New York Times Best Seller List."

"Your girlfriend?"

Sophie smiles.

Chapter 46

WHILE WAITING FOR Janie's call, Sophie and I check out her website and learn she's ghosted a dozen best-sellers. When the call comes in it comes to my cell phone instead of Sophie's house phone.

We look at each other, thinking the same thing. I forgot to remove the battery after hanging up with Ben.

I check the caller ID. "Unknown," I say.

"It's got to be Janie," she says.

"We didn't give Paul Small my cell phone number," I say.

The phone keeps ringing.

"I'm not going to answer it," I say. "This is too creepy. How would Janie get my personal cell phone number?"

"Ask her."

"No. I'm not dealing with anyone who can do that. If this is Janie, we're finding a different ghostwriter."

Just then, Sophie's house phone rings. It's suddenly noisy, both phones ringing at the same time.

"I'll answer mine if you'll answer yours!" she says, dashing to the kitchen.

"Too late," I holler. "Mine just went to voice mail."

Sophie answers her phone. Though I'm still on the couch in the den, I can hear enough to know she's talking to Janie Ramirez. While she's doing that, I check my voice mail.

And slide off the couch to the floor.

And nearly pass out.

When Sophie comes back to check on me, I'm sitting on the floor, shaking. She sees the tears streaming down my face.

"What on earth happened?"

I shudder, and point to my cell phone.

"It's him!" I say.

"Who, Ben?"

I shake my head.

She says, "Roy?"

I shake my head again.

"Who, Dani?"

"*ManChild*."

Chapter 47

SOPHIE PICKS UP my cell phone and puts it on speaker. Then replays the message:

> *"Hi Dani, this is ManChild. You don't know me yet, but we'll meet soon, you can count on that! I've been camped out in your yard all this time, waiting for you to call your husband, and you finally did! Call the police if you want, but I left after grabbing your signal. I know you think you're too old for me, but I like to think there's a bit of child in all of us. With that in mind, I'm going to capture you, Dani, just like Colin Tyler Hicks captured you years ago. And when I do, I'm going to strap you down and probe every orifice of your body until I find the little child that's hiding in you. Where do you think I'll find her?"*

"Holy shit!" Sophie says.

She yanks the battery out of my cell phone, runs through the house, locking doors, checking windows. Then sits by my side on the floor and holds me, and strokes my hair.

"What's with the creepy voice?" she says. "It sounds like he's talking through some sort of voice-altering device."

"He's gonna get me," I say.

"No. We'll get through this."

I say, "Sofe, I can't involve you in this. He'll kill you."

"You'll go back into witness protection," she says. "You'll change your name again, and move away. And I'll come with you. We'll start a new life."

Some time goes by, then I give her a weak smile. "Okay, so you're more romantic than me," I say. "But no, you can't run off and change your name. That's insane. You've got a life, a career. And anyway, you're well-known. People could track us down easily."

"We could cut and dye our hair and get a plastic surgeon to give us new faces."

"Watch a lot of TV, do you?" I say.

"I'm not going to lose you, Dani. If he gets you, he gets both of us."

"I won't put you in that kind of danger."

"I'll call Uncle Sal. He'll give us bodyguards."

"Is that how you want to live?"

"Hell yeah! Long as I'm with you."

Some more time passes.

"You'd resent me before long," I say.

"I'll resent you more if you leave me. And don't tell me we can't be together because you're married, because that marriage of yours is *bullshit!*"

I look at her and say, "Why don't you tell me how you *really* feel?"

She gives me a defiant look and says, "I'm not taking it back. Your marriage is a sham! It's bullshit. I said it, and I'll stand by it."

A moment passes, and suddenly Sophie and I burst into laughter. Then she says, "Seriously, what are we going to do about *ManChild?*"

"*Fuck ManChild!*" I say. "And fuck the witness protection program!"

"And fuck Ben Davis!" Sophie says.

I grin at her.

"Figure of speech," she says. Then adds, "What made *you* so bold all of a sudden? Ten minutes ago you were shaking like a leaf."

"Ten minutes ago I was in shock. That stupid message took me by surprise. Now I realize it's a hoax."

"The phone call?"

"Yeah."

"Tell me."

"Someone's fucking with me."

"What do you mean?"

"In real life, kidnappers don't call to warn you."

"They don't?"

"No. They have to rely on the element of surprise. Not only that, but *ManChild* is too smart to leave a voice message. And even if he did, he'd have no reason to disguise his voice."

"Unless you knew him."

"Exactly. And even if he knows how to steal a cell signal, he couldn't blend in with the reporters all this time, with signal-stealing equipment set up, hour after hour."

"So the person who called has to be someone you know."

"And it has to be someone who knows my cell phone number. Someone who enjoys seeing me squirm. Someone who threatened me recently, just to see me sweat."

"Roy?"

"Roy."

"You're positive?"

"One hundred percent."

She nods. "But just for safety's sake, let's don't power up your cell phone, okay?"

"Okay."

"Should you warn Ben?"

"Ben will be fine."

"You're sure?"

"Roy and *ManChild* have no reason to hurt Ben. Not to mention there are a hundred people surrounding the house. There's no way anyone could get to him."

"In the movies, the killer always finds a way to get in the house."

"Ben will be fine."

"You really think that was Roy?"

"I do."

"That's harassment, Dani. You should call your police boyfriend and report him."

"You mean Patrick Aub?"

Sophie laughs.

"What?"

"Just thinking a funny thought," she says.

"What?"

"Dani Aub!"

"Don't *even!*" I say, laughing.

Chapter 48

AN HOUR LATER we're lying on opposite ends of Sophie's couch, painting each other's toe nails.

"This is Ben's idea of what women would do when they're alone together," I say.

"He's right."

"This one time, maybe."

"Speaking of Ben, you're not going back to him."

I take a deep breath and let it out slowly. Then ask, "What did Janie Ramirez say about the book?"

"Change the subject all you want. But just so you know, we're definitely going to talk about this. Because you absolutely cannot go back to Ben's house."

"*Our* house."

"Whatever. Forget about Roy for a minute. Everyone knows where you live now. *ManChild* knows where you live. If he or some other kook decides to come after you some day, you'd be a sitting duck."

"What did Janie say about the ghostwriting idea?"

She scowls at me for changing the subject again, but says, "She agreed to read the manuscript tonight, said we could call her tomorrow morning."

Sophie jumps up."

"Where you going?"

"I forgot to send Janie the manuscript!"

By the time our nails are dry and we can't speak a full sentence without yawning, it's two a.m. Sophie says, "Can we sleep in the same bed tonight, or are you still married?"

"Still married."

"Aren't you afraid?"

"Of you? Terrified."

"I'm serious, Dani."

"Me too, Sofe."

Chapter 49

"WHAT'S YOUR OPINION of Ben's manuscript?" I ask Janie Ramirez via speaker phone, after introducing myself.

"It's well-written, but it's not the story people want to read."

"Why not?"

"People want to know three things: how you were kidnapped, what happened to you in that basement, and how you got away. That's it. Start with the kidnapping, end with the precinct house. As a reader, that's all I want. Give me that, I'll be happy."

"How long would it take to write my version?" I ask.

"We can self-publish your book and get it out before Ben signs a publishing contract. Four weeks, max."

"Aren't you forgetting something?"

"What's that?"

"I haven't written a book yet."

"It's been written, Dani," she says, "indelibly, in your brain. It just hasn't been written *down*."

"Excuse me," I say, shaking my head. "Did you just say four *weeks*? We can't write a book in four weeks. It took Ben almost a year."

"Ben padded the story. Remember, we're telling the story people want to hear. They don't want to hear how you grew up, or what treasures you kept under your bed when you were five. They don't want to know you were popular in school or if your parents fought at night."

"They don't?"

"Not unless those things came up in conversations between you and Hicks, or occupied your thoughts in the basement."

"I like it," Sophie says.

"Me too," I say.

"Good," Janie says. "When can we meet?"

"I might be bisexual," I say.

"Excuse me?"

Sophie says, "What made you blurt that out?"

I shrug. "I'm married to Ben, but Sophie and I kissed yesterday."

There's dead silence from both Janie and Sophie.

"I just wanted you to be aware of that," I say.

"In case it makes a difference," I add.

Finally, Janie says, "Are you planning to make a pass at me?"

I laugh. "No, of course not!"

"Then why would it make a difference?"

"I don't know. I just wanted it on the table."

"She's constantly blurting out inappropriate things," Sophie says. "It's part of her charm."

"It is?" I say.

"It's one of your most endearing qualities."

I wonder what that says about me. Then I realize Janie hasn't responded. "Janie? Are you still there?"

"I can't wait to meet you both," she says. "Your place or mine?"

Sophie says, "Ours."

"I need to warn you about something," I say. "There's a guy, *ManChild*, who's trying to find me. If he does, he's going to kidnap and kill me. So there could be danger."

"Sounds exciting!" Janie says.

Chapter 50

WE DECIDE JANIE will fly to Nashville this afternoon, and Sophie will pick her up at the airport. She and I will work together by day, and she'll spend the nights at a nearby motel. Janie says she'll only need a few days in person, and can follow up with phone calls later in the week.

My new attorney, Paul Small, calls and says he's not comfortable seeking an injunction to stop Ben's book from being published. Worse, he says I need to inform Ben of my plan to write my own book, because the publishing houses bidding for Ben's book will expect full disclosure. If they don't get it, they could sue us, claiming my book hurt Ben's sales.

"And it would," Paul says. "In fact, when they hear about your book they won't want Ben's."

"My full disclosure could cost him a million dollars?" I ask.

"Yes. But remember, Ben never discussed his book with you. And he paid someone to blow your cover."

"So?"

"You owe him nothing, Dani."

"I owe him for other things."

"He'll be fine. He's still your husband."

"What's that mean?"

"It means he's entitled to half the earnings from your book."

"Maybe I should rethink my marital status," I say.

"If you're planning to divorce, you should work out an agreement before you publish."

"If we're divorcing, do I have to tell him I'm writing my own book?"

"Yes."

"That comes under full disclosure?"

"It does."

"Do I have to tell him my book will be out in four weeks?"

"No."

"Good, because Ben will assume I'm all talk."

"Do you want a divorce?"

"I'm trying to decide. I might be bisexual."

"Excuse me?"

"I'm giving you full disclosure."

"I'm not sure I follow."

"I kissed Sophie yesterday."

"Sophie Alexander? My client?"

"Yes. And I liked it."

"Well..."

"Well, what?"

"I'm not sure how to respond to that," Paul says.

"Is it okay that I kissed her?"

"It's okay with *me*. But why would you feel the need to tell me that?"

"I'm telling everyone."

"Well, I'm not a divorce attorney, but I wouldn't feel obligated to mention it to Ben."

"Even under full disclosure?"

"You like saying full disclosure, don't you?"

"When I learn a new phrase I like to use it as often as possible."

"Well, as I say, I'm not a divorce attorney. But if you've exchanged a single kiss, I'm not sure Ben needs to know."

"What if Sophie and I play *teacher's pet*?"

"Are you having sport with me?"

"Uh...yes. A little."

"Well, if you and Sophie play *teacher's pet*, you know what I'll expect, right?"

"Full disclosure?"

"That's right. And photos, if you've got them."

"You're funny."

Chapter 51

SOPHIE HAD PREVIOUSLY scheduled a meeting with a young country singer for this afternoon, and asks if I want her to cancel it.

"Of course not!" I say. "You can't change your whole life to accommodate me."

"Want to come with me? You can wear the auburn wig and use a pencil to color your eyebrows. Give you black lipstick, make you look gothic."

"Maybe I should just put a sheet over my head and cut two eye holes."

"Fine, be like that. But you can't stay locked away forever."

"What I really want is to call Pat Aub and tell him Roy pretended to be ManChild."

"I know you think your phone is safe, but please don't use it. Just in case."

"I can't use your house phone, either. Because Pat could find out where I am."

"While I'm out I'll swing by Wal-Mart, buy a prepaid phone. You can use that one to call Pat."

"Thanks, Sofe."

She leaves, and I turn on the TV and see the media frenzy hasn't abated. My sudden disappearance is fueling stories and lots of speculation. At the top of the hour, the twenty-four-hour news channel replays a press conference Ben held on our doorstep last night, during which he told the world he established contact with me. He said I'm fine, in good spirits, and he wants them to respect my privacy. As I watch and listen to my husband's appearance on national TV, it strikes me how much credit he's taking for making sure I'm safe. It's also clear he really enjoys his time in the spotlight, although he looks dreadful. He's pale, gaunt, and looks like he hasn't slept in days. I wonder if he still has the flu bug. A dozen news people pepper him with questions, and he fields them long after he could have walked away. At one point he tries to get in a plug for his book, but the reporters sidestep him, preferring to ask more salacious questions, including:

"Is there any truth to the rumor Dani's in rehab?"

His answer: "What? Rehab? Who told you that?"

"There was a reported sighting of Dani near Roswell, New Mexico. Can you confirm or deny she's being held in a bunker for her own protection?"

His answer: "Confirm or deny the report? Or that she's in Roswell?"

I switch the station and see a famous TV psychologist giving his professional opinion about what's going on in my mind right now. He offers his counseling services free of charge, and reminds the audience he's had remarkable success with celebrities.

I'm a celebrity?

I switch to an entertainment channel and see members of the Hollywood elite being interviewed on the red carpet of some movie premiere that took place last night:

"Lisbon," says the lady with the mike, "where do you think Dani Ripper's hiding?"

Her answer: "She's probably in an abandoned bowling alley, like the one in my new movie, *Twilight Bowling for Zombies*. It opens Friday."

"Fairfax, if they make a movie, who should play Dani Ripper?"

Her answer: "I'd play her, if the producers agree to my demands. I expect a forty-foot trailer, decorated in bronze. Everything inside must be bronze, including the furniture, walls, ceiling, and carpet. Everything except the toilet paper. That has to be mauve. And I want mauve rose petals sprinkled in the bowl every time I flush."

"Well, that certainly sounds reasonable," the lady with the mike gushes, and moves on to the next celebrity.

"We're on the carpet with the world's most famous female rapper, Naomi Trapper. Naomi, what advice do you have for Dani Ripper?"

Her answer: "Stay put, child! Wherever the hell you are, don't come here! 'Cause this place is *bleep*!"

To me, Naomi's answer seems the most practical.

Chapter 52

SATURDAY AFTERNOON, SUNDAY, AND MONDAY

JANIE LOOKS EXACTLY like her publicity photo—if you wad it into a ball, then try to smooth it out again.

"Sorry for my appearance," she says. "I had a bad flight."

"Turbulence?"

"In-flight meal."

"Need a bathroom?"

"I think I'm okay," she says, "now that I've coughed up my spleen at the airport. How are you holding up?"

"I'm good. But I need to make a quick call."

Sophie gives me the disposable phone and I call Pat. When he answers, I say, "Pat, this is Dani."

"Wow! Call me back in five minutes."

He hangs up.

Janie and Sophie head for the dining room table, and chat while Janie unpacks her laptop. I call Pat again, and he spends a great deal of time telling me how shocked he was to hear about my true identity. I tell him about Ben hiring Roy to break the news to the press.

"That sucks, Dani, but I'm not sure it constitutes a crime," Pat says.

I tell Pat how Roy came to my office and threatened me, and now he's posing as *ManChild*, and threatening me again.

"That definitely constitutes harrassment," Pat says, "so be sure to save the voice message. What's Roy's full name?"

"He was posing as Roy Burroughs, but I can't remember his real name. Ben can tell you. He works—or used to work—in the drama department at Riverton College."

"I'll have someone look into it," he says.

"What does that mean, exactly?"

"I'll have a talk with Ben and find out who this guy is and where I can find him. In the meantime, don't use your personal cell phone."

"I know. That's why I'm using a disposable one right now."

"Smart girl. Are you somewhere safe?"

"Yes."

"I won't ask where. Just...be careful, okay?"

"I will. And Pat?"

"Yeah?"

"Make Roy stop bothering me, okay?"

"Count on it."

We hang up, and I turn off the phone and take a seat at the dining room table across from Janie Ramirez.

"Seems like the whole world is talking about you," she says.

"But *you* won't say anything, right?"

"No one will know we've spoken until the book comes out."

"That's when you need to be extra careful," I say. "It's possible the real *ManChild* might come after you, to make you tell where I am."

"Hopefully the police will have him in custody by then."

"And if not?"

"I'll get police protection."

"Good idea."

Janie says, "Any other questions before we start?"

"Just one. Should I get a divorce?"

"Yes, absolutely."

I laugh. "You don't even *know* me!"

She says, "You're here with Sophie instead of home with your husband. It appears you've already made your decision."

Sophie beams. "I like this lady!"

"She prepped you on the ride over, didn't she?" I say.

"I'm pleading the fifth," Janie says. "Let's get to work."

And with that, we begin the first of three marathon sessions. To my surprise, Janie wants to know every word spoken by Colin Tyler Hicks and me, from the moment I entered the basement to the moment I left.

"He talked a lot about other kidnap victims," I say. "I remember most of the names, but not all of them."

"I'll do an online search tonight and make a list," she says. "Tomorrow we can see if you left anyone out. For now, let's get the dialog right."

"Which dialog?"

"Start with what you remember word for word. Then we'll fill in the rest."

"You don't want me to start at the beginning?"

"No. I want you to start with the most memorable."

"What about the bad things that happened?"

"We'll get to that and leave nothing out. But the dialog is crucial."

"Ben's book didn't have *any* dialog between me and Hicks."

"The readers want to know what was said in that basement, and how it was said. It personalizes the experience for them. Makes them feel they're in the room with you. Otherwise it'll come across cold and clinical, like a crime scene report."

Sophie and I exchange a look.

She says, "I think we've got the right ghostwriter."

Over the next five hours I tell Janie everything I can remember. She comes back the next morning and we put in twelve full hours. She comes back Monday and we do another twelve hours. Then, at eight p.m., she says we're done. After she leaves, Sophie makes popcorn and turns on the TV and we learn that my husband, Ben Davis, is dead.

Chapter 53

TUESDAY

ACCORDING TO SOPHIE I screamed and cried for fourteen hours straight. That's not entirely true, but it's close. I remember Sophie called Pat Aub to confirm Ben's death, and he did. He also said he tried to call my cell phone twenty times, and because he couldn't track me down, police lost hours trying to get permission to enter my residence. Cops can't claim a door is unlocked when a hundred reporters are documenting their every move. Pat asked Sophie's name and address, but she refused to give it. He insisted I get on the line, and she told him to kiss her ass. But Pat's always been good to me, so I took the phone.

He said, "Are you okay, Dani?"

"Of course not. It's all my fault."

"What are you talking about?"

"Ben's dead because of me. I should have warned him about the message on my cell phone."

"He wasn't murdered, Dani."

"*ManChild* got him, Pat. He killed Ben, hoping to find me."

"According to the coroner, it didn't go down that way."

"*ManChild* killed him. And it's my fault."

"It's time you told me where you are. We'll need the address. We also need full details on the woman who's with you."

"I'm not ready to be found yet."

He paused. "You need to rethink that. For now I'm willing to say you refused to divulge the information."

"Okay."

"What I really need is your permission to search the premises."

I was loopy with grief and shock, but said, "You obviously searched the house when you found Ben's body."

"You know how this works, Dani. I need your official permission."

"Then yes, conduct a full search. Tear the place apart. I'll agree to anything that will help you catch *ManChild*."

"We'll videotape the search, and I'll be there the whole time. Please keep this phone on, okay? I really need to be able to contact you."

I thanked him and ended the call. Then removed the phone's battery because if I didn't, there'd be cops here within an hour.

The conversation with Pat was one of my few lucid moments on this miserable day.

I remember wanting to be alone, in a small place, like when Collin Tyler Hicks locked me in his basement nine years ago. Maybe that's why I found myself curled up on the shower floor in Sophie's guest bathroom, getting pelted by hot water. When the water turned cold, I got up and went somewhere else. An hour later I was back in the shower, using up some more of Sophie's hot water.

I remember Sophie sobbing outside my bedroom door, asking if she could come in. I remember her saying over and over that the media was calling for me to turn myself in to the police because if I didn't, they were going to put out a warrant for my arrest. They needed to know my whereabouts and any information I might have that could aid their investigation of Ben's death.

I remember Sophie telling me over and over if I didn't establish contact, the police were going to think I was involved. So I finally called them, and two officers showed up and waited respectfully for me to compose myself before driving me to the station.

On the way, I'm asked, "Was Ben on any prescription medications you know about?"

"No. He's in perfect health...*Was* in perfect health," I amend, and start crying.

"Any illicit drug use you're aware of?"

"No, of course not."

"Besides you and Ben, who else has keys to your house?"

It suddenly dawns on me I'm being interviewed by the police.

Chapter 54

I'M IN A police car with two chatty police officers.

"Should I get a lawyer?" I ask.

"You're not a suspect," one of them says. "Your husband's body was found by two officers of the Cincinnati police department. He doesn't appear to have been murdered."

The police have their own theory, but I'm convinced Ben was murdered by *ManChild*.

The other cop says, "There were no signs of an intruder. All the doors and windows were locked. Countless reporters and police were on the property at all times, and no one was seen entering or exiting the residence, except the few times Ben came out to talk to the press."

"Then how did he die?"

"What we're hearing, according to the coroner, is heart attack, or natural causes."

"That's crazy. Ben was only thirty-eight."

They start to say something, but look at each other and decide they've already said more than their pay grade warrants.

Earlier, before the police arrived, Sophie called Paul Small. Paul called a defense attorney, Chris Fist, who agreed to represent me during the formal interview. After meeting Chris at the station, we go into an interrogation room and meet a detective named Marco Polo.

"I'm going to have to read that on your ID," Chris says.

The detective says, "My ID will tell you I'm Marco Polomo. But—"

"All your life you've had the nickname."

He nods. "You should've been there the first time I went to a public swimming pool. I was six. Thought everyone there was yelling at me. I kept hollering back, 'What do you *want?*'"

After setting some ground rules, Polomo brings us up to speed on the current developments. He says the case belongs to Cincinnati, and he's not privy to all the details. But Cincy's granting unprecedented cooperation because I'm under the Nashville PD's protective custody.

I say, "What have they found out about my husband's death?"

"It's too early to rule out suicide or foul play," Polomo says, "since Ben was found in a fetal position clutching his chest. But there was no foaming of the mouth, or vomit, or other outward or obvious signs of poisoning. They've done a toxicology report and are waiting on the results. According to his doctor, Ben wasn't taking prescription drugs, and

Cincy PD found none at the premises, nor any evidence of illicit drug use."

"Ben was healthy as a horse," I say. "Someone killed him. And I think it's someone I know."

I then proceed to tell him everything I know about Roy, except for the part about how Roy and Carter Teague paid me five thousand dollars to take my clothes off at the Brundage Hotel.

"You have the cell phone with you?"

I retrieve the cell and battery, but Chris Fist tells me to put them back in my purse.

Detective Polomo frowns. "We'd really like to hear that prank call," he says.

"You'd also love full access to her cell phone, wouldn't you?"

"We can order cell phone records."

"I'm sure you already have them. But there's a lot of personal information on the actual phone you don't need to see unless you're planning to arrest my client."

"Will you play just the prank call so we can get it on tape? We're on the same side here, counselor."

Chris and I go out to his car and listen to the prank call Roy made. Chris asks me about Sophie, Ben, and Roy, and says, "There's more to this Roy connection than you're telling me, and I hope you're not hiding something that's going to come back and bite you in the butt."

"There's nothing else," I say.

"If that's true, I suppose we can play the tape for them."

We go back inside and they record the prank call.

"I believe this is the man who killed my husband," I say.

Polomo says, "Well, as I say, they think it's highly unlikely. I expect your first hunch was correct. This is the man your husband hired to break the news to the press. He threatened you earlier, he's threatening you now. There are a lot of sicko's out there, Ms. Ripper, and this guy obviously gets off on threatening women."

He pauses.

Chris says, "Anything else?"

Polomo says, "The home search your client authorized uncovered some unusual items."

He suddenly has my full attention.

"What sorts of items?"

"They won't say. But what *could* they mean by that?"

I say, "My computer might have some odd searches. I've subscribed to some sites that are known to be—"

Chris interrupts, saying, "I'm instructing my client not to answer any further questions at this time."

Polomo frowns and says, "She can speak freely. She's not a suspect. Ben Davis died of natural causes, not murder. And even if it turns out he *was* murdered, Sophie Alexander has provided your client with an air-tight alibi. Not to mention the whole world knows what she looks like. She couldn't have been anywhere near the house without being spotted."

"Detective Polomo," Chris says. "How many clients have gone to jail after being assured they weren't suspects?"

Polomo frowns.

Chris says, "You mentioned Ms. Ripper is under police protection. What does that include?"

JOHN LOCKE

"We're willing to put a uniform inside Sophie's house and two more on her property."

"It won't do any good," I say. "If Roy could get past all those reporters at my house, he can get past three cops at Sophie's."

"When it comes to security, there's a big difference between reporters and cops," Polomo says, and he's right. Because the next morning Sophie and I are still alive, despite the fact there are more than two hundred reporters and photographers camped outside her house.

Oh, and Uncle Sal called. Yup. He called Sophie the minute the news broke that I was staying with his niece. He wanted to know the connection. She said she was in love with me!

While all this took place, Sophie pulled me into the farthest corner away from our guards and put Sal on speaker, so I could hear him say, "Aw, shit!"

Sophie said, "What, you don't approve of my lifestyle?"

Sal said, "Don't go all—whatcha call—Ellen on me. There's other stuff going on. Jeez."

"What other stuff?"

"Look, I wanna help, but your place is swarming with cops."

"I'll be all right."

"This is causing problems."

"I don't understand how Dani's being here affects you in the slightest possible way."

"Look, I gotta go. You sure you're all right?"

"I'm fine."

"I'll be in touch," he says.

Sophie hangs up.

"He sounds like a charmer," I say.

She sighs. "It'd be so much easier if he worked in a deli."

Chapter 55

WEDNESDAY

WITH THE CERTAIN knowledge I'm in Sophie's house, the neighborhood has been overrun. In response, the police have beefed up security around the house, and stationed a number of plainclothes cops among the crowd. The FBI has gotten in on the action, as well. Their reasoning? *ManChild* is an unsolved kidnapping case, and I've been threatened. Apparently that's reason enough to set up a mini command center in Sophie's kitchen.

Though I'm convinced the real *ManChild* isn't after me, word has gotten out about the taped message, and the city's in a panic over it. My best protection against *ManChild* appears to be the paparazzi and reporters desperately hoping to capture his image on film. Thousands of minutes of footage are taken and analyzed, and the police and FBI seem powerless to keep the reporters and photographers at bay.

Outside of Nashville, I'm the big attraction. According to news reports, twelve thousand reporters and photographers are expected to descend upon the city in the next twenty-four hours. The police have begun barricading the streets. Homeowners living within four blocks of Sophie's house are being forced to show ID in order to enter or exit their own neighborhoods. The FBI has discussed taking Sophie and me into protective custody at an undisclosed location.

Getting protective personnel into the house is a major production, but bringing in food is such a terrifying prospect, Sophie and I refuse to eat anything that isn't already in her pantry, which makes for some really crappy meals. We don't sleep much, what with the reporters screaming at us day and night, and news helicopters flying overhead. On TV, the biggest names in show business are jockeying to attend Ben's funeral, hoping to be photographed with the grieving widow, a display of opportunism that particularly turns my stomach.

Due to security issues, and continued questioning by the Nashville police and FBI, I'm unable to make the arrangements for Ben's funeral in Cincinnati Friday, except in the most general way, so his father and mother travel from Florida to Cincinnati to coordinate the details for me.

Chapter 56

THURSDAY

AS THE FUNERAL draws near there are tears and more tears, and I feel horrible for having been such a rotten wife to Ben. Though the police and FBI are firmly against it, Sophie and I are determined to attend Ben's funeral tomorrow.

Sophie is contacted by country music star Betty Tilden, who recorded two of Sophie's songs. She offers the use of her private jet in return for accompanying us to Cincinnati for the funeral and having the opportunity to meet and travel with me. The police think flying into a private airport is the safest way for us to get there, so I accept Betty's generous offer. Betty asks if there's anything special we'd like her to have the caterers put on the plane, and Sophie tells her anything she brings would be a blessing, since we've eaten nearly all the food in her pantry.

Chapter 57

FRIDAY

THE FIRST PUBLIC pictures taken of me since the news broke show Sophie and me surrounded by police, with coats over our heads. They take us to a private aviation company where Betty's jet is standing by, complete with two security guards. We take off and arrive in Cincinnati forty-five minutes later. Sophie, Betty, me, and the two guards exit the jet, walk twenty feet, and climb into the stretch limousine Betty ordered, and head to the funeral home in total silence.

The funeral is crushingly awful, especially the part where Ben's mother publicly spits in my face and screams, "My son is dead because of you!" She's right, of course, so I just stand there with her spit on my face until Sophie forces me into the ladies' room. After cleaning me up, she retouches my makeup. I don't care how I look. I'm numb with guilt and sadness.

We exit the ladies' room and find Pat Aub standing just outside the door. He says hi, introduces himself to Sophie, and says he's here for us, and he's not alone. Dozens of local policemen and women have volunteered their time to ensure the funeral service remains uninterrupted by the media. I thank him and ask him to thank the others for me. His gaze lingers.

"You're okay?" he says.

"No."

He nods. "Dani, when all this is over, if you ever feel like—"

"I know, Pat. We'll see."

He leans over and kisses my cheek, then turns and walks back down the hall to guard the side door.

"He's cute," Sophie whispers.

"You think?"

She leans into my ear and whispers, "Wouldn't it be funny if Pat turned out to be *ManChild*?"

"No."

Ben's ex, Erica, attempts to talk to me, but there's not much she can say. Her son—Ben's son—doesn't seem very upset, but of course, some could say the same about me, since I'm not publicly sobbing or gnashing my teeth. I probably would, but three days of crying, no sleep, and constant questioning by the police, has taken its toll.

Somehow we get through it, Sophie and me, and when we leave, a line of police are holding back a throng of enthusiastic onlookers. Many are holding signs and shouting words of encouragement.

Not everyone is sympathetic. One sign reads, DANI: NOW THAT YOU'RE SINGLE, WILL YOU MARRY ME?

No, asshole, I won't.

We ride back to the private airstrip with our new best friend, Betty Tilden, who feels comfortable enough to negotiate an album of songs to be written by Sophie. I'm appalled, but keep it to myself, realizing that for others, the funeral represented little more than a few moments to pause and reflect, and life has already gone on. Amazingly, Betty asks if I'd consider singing backup on some of the tracks. That's an easy no, but I don't want to ruin things for Sophie, so I tell her I'll think about it.

When we climb into Betty's jet I'm shocked to see two huge boxes of groceries secured to the couch! She'd ordered ahead. While we were at the funeral, Betty had her pilots fetch the boxes to ensure Sophie and I would be well-provisioned upon our return. She turned out to be pretty thoughtful after all.

Chapter 58

SATURDAY

LIKE GAYLE KING and Oprah, Sophie Alexander has become famous for being my friend. Her phone rings constantly as TV stations and newspapers across the country attempt to go through her to get to me. She contacts her agent, Charlie Yang, and I agree to let him represent me if he'll handle all inquiries. Within hours of Charlie's press release announcing our new working relationship, Sophie's phone goes quiet, and everyone who wants me calls him. Even the publishing houses contact Charlie to ask if I'll approve Ben's book for publication. I'm a nightmare client for Charlie, because I refuse to discuss any offers until Janie finishes our book.

Charlie didn't prepare me for what I see on TV tonight. Apparently I've been offered a million dollars to appear nude in a girly magazine. I feel violated, somehow, even though a couple of weeks ago I got naked in a hotel room for five thousand bucks.

"Guess I've hit the big time," I say.

"I'm sorry, Dani," Sophie says.

Chapter 59

SUNDAY

SPEAKING OF SOPHIE, she's been amazing. She's my rock, my best friend. We're sleeping in the same bed now, but there's no kissing, touching, or even a hint of playfulness. I'm emotionally spent, and Sophie's okay with it.

Every morning I apologize for crying half the night, but she says she's got it better than a newborn's parents.

"At least I don't have to change diapers," she says.

I'm most gratified by the fact she's not hovering. She never asks if I'm okay, never follows me around, never goes out of her way to do things for me. She talks sparingly, and has a wonderful instinct for what I need right now, which is normalcy.

The FBI agents have moved out of the house and been replaced by a police security detail. Of course, they've explained they can't continue providing security indefinitely, and Sophie and I are trying to decide what to do when we're left completely alone. We're convinced the paparazzi will break into her house and photograph us to death if *ManChild* or some other kook doesn't get to us first.

Chapter 60

TWO THINGS HAPPEN today.

First, Janie Ramirez calls to say she's completed the first draft of our book, which she's fittingly titled, *The Little Girl Who Got Away*. She says she'll send the manuscript by email. I thank her for her time and for the flowers she sent to the funeral home.

Second, less than a minute after Janie hangs up, I get a call from my new attorney, Chris Fist.

"Have they got there yet?" he says.

"Who are we talking about?"

"The FBI. If they get there before me, tell them to wait, and don't say anything. I'll be there in ten minutes."

I start to ask why they're coming, but he's already hung up.

Moments later Detective Marco Polomo enters the house with two FBI agents. He introduces them, and asks Sophie to leave us alone.

"You may as well let Sophie stay, because first, it's her house, and second, I'm going to tell her everything the minute you leave."

Polomo gives in. "Where can we sit and talk?"

"My attorney just called. He's on his way."

"Figures," one of the G men says.

We twiddle our thumbs until Chris shows up. Then we sit in the den and Agent Chase opens a manila envelope and places a photograph on the coffee table in front of me.

"Recognize this?" he says.

Chris says, "You can answer the question honestly."

"No."

"No you don't recognize it?"

"I don't. Nor do I have any idea what it is," I say.

"It's a voice altering device."

"Like the kind Roy used when he left that message?"

"Yes. Except this one was found in your home."

"My home? Where?"

"Ben's desk drawer."

He pulls out another photo and sets it before me. It's a picture of what appears to be a decorative, handcrafted wooden keepsake box. The wood appears to be walnut, and features angled sides and contrasting box joint corners made of oak or ash. It's exquisitely crafted. Someone has taken great care to polish it to a high luster. It appears to be half the size of a shoe box, and has a keyhole.

"Ever seen this?"

255

"No, but it's gorgeous."

"It was found in your basement, in a cardboard box, under a pile of old college essays and lesson plans."

"When?"

"The day you authorized the Cincinnati police to conduct a thorough search of your home."

"That was a *week* ago! Why are you just now showing me this?"

"What difference does it make?" he says. "You've either seen it or you haven't."

"She hasn't," Chris Fist says.

"It took us two days to find the key," Agent Chase says.

"Okay."

"Know where we found it?"

Chris says, "If she's never seen the box, how would she know where you found the key? Assuming there's a point to these questions, can you get to it?"

Agent Chase gives Chris a long, hard look. Then turns to me and says, "You know the small, framed photo of you on Ben's desk, to the left of his computer? You're younger, big smile, wearing a yellow blouse. There's a horse fence and a tree in the background."

I blot the tears from my eyes.

"I know the picture," I say. "It was Ben's favorite."

"The key was hidden between the photo and the backing, between two pieces of cardboard."

Sophie says, "What's in the box?"

Chase says, "Glad you asked."

He pulls three photos from the manila envelope and spreads them out in front of me.

It takes me a moment to realize what I'm seeing.
Then I start screaming.

Chapter 61

I WANT TO turn my head away, but can't.

Sophie's hand flies across the coffee table and connects against the side of Agent Chase's face so hard it knocks him back.

"What the fuck's the matter with you?" she screams, and cocks her arm to slap the other guy just for being there. But Chris Fist lunges and manages to restrain her.

"Your client just assaulted a federal agent!" Chase yells, rubbing the side of his face.

"Fuck you!" Sophie says, trying to squirm out of Chris's grip so she can slap Chase again.

"I could have you arrested for this!" he says. "Tell her, Mr. Fist."

Chris says, "First of all, Sophie's not my client. Second, she asked you a fair question. Why the hell would you ambush Dani with these photos? You think she hasn't been through enough in her twenty-four years?"

"Watch your tone, counselor."

"Watch yours, you piece of shit."

Sophie says, "Dani?"

...And everyone turns to me.

Chapter 62

I CAN'T STOP looking at the photos. The first one isn't so bad. It's a photo of the same box, with the lid open. There's some sort of cloth inside. No big deal, right?

The second photo shows the piece of cloth spread out beside the box. Only it's no longer a random piece of cloth.

It's a pair of blood-stained panties.

A little girl's panties.

And of course the third photo is a picture of little Jaqui Moreland.

She's naked, and her mouth is duct-taped. Her arms and legs are duct-taped so that she's lying spread-eagle on the floor. It's not clear what the tape is attached to outside the area of the photograph, nor is it important.

What's important is Jaqui's eyes. They're wide with terror.

Agent Chase says, "The photo's authentic. This is Jaqui Moreland, moments before her death. We're still waiting on the DNA results, but the panties match the description in her mother's original statement. By the way, we never disclosed Jaqui's panties were absent the crime scene."

I can't stop looking at the photo. I can barely see through my tears, but I can see enough.

"Put the photos away," Chris says.

It still hasn't dawned on me the significance of why they're showing me these photos. Then Agent Chase says, "We've spent the past week trying to decide if you had any knowledge your husband raped and killed Jaqui Moreland."

"*What?*"

I don't know why his words shocked me. For five minutes he's been showing me positive proof that my husband, Ben Davis, the man I tried so hard to love, was *ManChild*.

Now, suddenly, it makes sense.

According to Roy, Ben fell in love with me when he was twenty-nine.

Back then I was...

I was fifteen.

It fits.

But still. Ben?

"Maybe *ManChild* set him up," I say.

Chase says, "We lifted Ben's fingerprints off the photograph. The threatening call you received was made with a voice-altering device exactly like the one in Ben's home office."

"Why would Ben try to frighten me?" I ask, though Ben himself already gave me the answer. He was hoping the revelation about my identity, and the book deal, and my fear of *ManChild*, would drive me back into his arms.

I think about how Ben always compared our relationship to an orange in a vodka bottle. Like Sophie said, I was his prisoner.

I wonder why he allowed me to live.

Is it because I grew older than the age he liked to kill? Is it because he needed me by his side to keep others from being suspicious? Did he love me too much to kill me? Or was he planning to kill me when I returned from Sophie's?

I think about the days he spent helping Jaqui's family search for her. Up to ten hours a day he combed the woods and fields with the other volunteers. Colin Tyler Hicks attempted to do the same thing after abducting me. I saw a TV show where they claimed killers and kidnappers often volunteer to search for their victims, and are often the ones who "find" the bodies. Ben must have loved the irony of how hard I worked every day to catch the pervert who was living in my own home.

"I knew nothing about it," I tell Agent Chase. "I've spent endless time and money trying to catch *ManChild*. Everyone knows that."

"Which is exactly what made us suspicious," he says. "If you're trying to protect Ben Davis, what better cover could you possibly have than to act like you're spending every waking hour searching for Jaqui's killer?"

Chris says, "Do you have anything to charge her with, or were you just trying to get her reaction to the photos?"

"We were testing her reaction."

"And?"

"My professional opinion? She's either completely innocent, or one hell of an actress."

Chapter 63

TUESDAY MORNING

TODAY WHEN I wake up, Sophie's not in the room, but my cell phone is, and it's ringing.

"Hello?"

"Good news, Dani!" Chris Fist says.

"I could use some. What's up?"

"The police and FBI have cleared you of any wrongdoing."

"Did they establish a cause of death?"

"Ben died of heart failure. His autopsy showed a previously undetected congenital heart defect. It was like a time bomb waiting to go off, and any sudden exertion or stress could have triggered it. They think his recent bout with the flu weakened him, and the stress of being hounded by the media probably did him in."

"In a sense he killed himself?"

"In a very real sense. His heart couldn't take the stress of the media storm he, himself caused."

We talk until I hear a noise down the hall. Then I hang up and get out of bed to investigate. When I enter Sophie's room, I find her taping a cardboard box.

"What's up, Sofe?"

"I'm tossing some stuff away."

"What is it?"

"Nothing important."

"Show me."

She opens the lid, reaches her hand in the box, and pulls out some plaid schoolgirl skirts.

"What gives?" I say.

"Are you kidding me? After what happened yesterday with Jaqui's photos? I thought about the whole *teacher's pet* thing and wanted to vomit."

"Why?"

"My fantasy game isn't cute *or* sexy, it's perverted. I'm no higher up the food chain than Colin Tyler Hicks, or...*ManChild*."

"You can say Ben. I've accepted it."

"Well anyway, the skirts are going straight to Goodwill."

"Sofe."

"What?"

"There's a huge difference between *teacher's pet* and the other kinds of thoughts."

"There is?"

"Of course."

"Enlighten me," she says.

"Well...um..."

"Yes?"

"Okay, so nothing comes to mind. But I haven't had my coffee yet."

"Doesn't matter. I'm done with it."

"No more *teacher's pet?*"

"Never again. I can't believe I never saw the creep factor before yesterday."

I sigh.

"What?"

"I can't believe I've done this to you."

"What?"

"I've taken the fun out of something you enjoyed. It wasn't dirty, wasn't perverted. You played your games with grown women, yes?"

"Not *that* many women," she says.

"How many exactly?"

"Two. But I'll never be able to play it without thinking of that poor child. So I'm done."

"Just like that?"

"Just like that."

"That's so *sad*," I say.

She shrugs.

"No more sex games? Really, Sofe?"

"I didn't say *that*."

I look at her. "What do you mean?"

She enters the closet and comes out with a sparkly outfit in her hand and a smile on her face. "We can still play *casting couch!*"

Chapter 64

SOPHIE AND I spend the rest of the day reading Janie's manuscript. Then I call her to discuss the passages she highlighted, where she asked for additional input.

"I loved it," I say. "Thank you so much for all your hard work."

After I hang up Sophie says, "Did you mean that?"

"What?"

"You told her you loved the manuscript. Did you?"

"Yes. Didn't you?"

"It was very difficult for me to read."

"I know. But the way it's written is exactly what happened."

"You never told me Hicks said those things to you."

"I know. But it's a huge part of the story."

"Still."

I look into her eyes. They're welling with tears.

"What's wrong, Sofe?"

"I mean, it's really creepy."

"Yes."

Her eyes appear to have contained the tears, but she blinks, and suddenly half her face is wet.

She says, "I can't believe you went through all that. It's...I mean...I could never..."

"Never what?"

"Your attitude. It's...so perky. So bubbly. And positive."

"I survived."

"Yes."

"Colin Tyler Hicks took several years from me, but I've come all the way back. You helped."

"I did?"

"Yup."

She kisses my cheek. Then says, "Are you sure you're comfortable publishing it?"

"It's exactly what happened."

"I know, but still."

"I know, Sofe. But it's exactly what happened."

"Jesus, Dani."

Chapter 65

MONDAY

THE POLICE ARE gone now, and only a dozen reporters are hanging around. I doubt they've ever encountered anyone as stubborn as Sophie and me. We haven't so much as opened a curtain since returning from the funeral ten days ago. We've gone through the original provisions Betty's pilots secured for us in Cincinnati, but she stops by nearly every day to work with Sophie on the songs for her new album. When she does, her bodyguards always bring at least one basket of goodies for us.

Betty heard me singing in the kitchen a few days ago, and appears to have lost interest in using me for backup vocals.

The girls are working hard at the piano in the den, so the bodyguards open a dining room curtain to scowl menacingly at the reporters outside. Pat Aub calls and asks if I'm still planning to be in Cincinnati tomorrow to meet with the attorney to review Ben's *Last Will and Testament*. I tell him that's the plan, and mention Sophie's coming with me. Pat offers to meet us at the airport and take us to lunch.

Pat's a good man and a good friend, but I decline his offer. It wouldn't be right to lead him on, since I know what he wants, and I'm not feeling the connection.

Chapter 66

WEDNESDAY,
NINE DAYS LATER

WITH EACH PASSING day I steadily detach myself from the emotional connection I once had with Ben. I'd been living with a perverted monster, and have willed myself to hate him. I take great comfort knowing we never had children together. Though Ben left me the house, I signed it over to his son. I refuse to step inside it, even to retrieve my personal items.

Nothing sexual has happened between me and Sophie yet, and she's gone back to sleeping in the upstairs bedroom down the hall just like she used to. That said, I'm starting to look at her a little differently. Last night when we climbed the stairs to go to bed, I accidently-on-purpose dropped a hairbrush on the floor, and peeked down her pajama shirt when she bent over to pick it up for me.

It was an experiment, to see if viewing her nakedness would have an effect on me. I could have gotten my answer by offering to have sex with her, but that would take us past the point of no return. The worst thing I could ever do to Sophie is wind up in bed with her and not be interested.

Since I've told you this much about the experiment, I suppose I owe you a summary of the results. When I glimpsed her breasts, my pulse quickened, and I felt my face flush. A few minutes later, I must've made a sound from my bed, because Sophie called out, "Is everything okay?"

Everything was.

Chapter 67

TWO WEEKS LATER...

FUNNY HOW THE mind works.

You get a visit at your office from a guy like Roy who knows about your past. He makes some claims about your husband having a fixation on a fifteen-year-old girl, and even though you know it doesn't make sense, he's created a wedge of doubt because he's right about you being The Little Girl Who Got Away.

Then you get a hinky call from *ManChild*, the killer-rapist you've been trying to track down, but that sort of call doesn't fit his profile. Then your very healthy husband dies, after complaining about being "sick as a dog" for several days, and all this evidence turns up, complete with a dead girl's panties and Ben's fingerprints.

Everyone's rushing to judgment, including you, because the cops and Feds are convinced, and that's what they do for a living.

So you accept the fact you've been living with a killer-rapist and you're glad you never had his children. Not that you can have children in the first place. But you're happy to get it all behind you and move on with your life. After all, you've got a budding relationship with a wonderful lady with whom you're falling in love. It would be so easy to buy the official explanations, and trust the evidence.

But what if Ben didn't do it?

If he didn't do it, shouldn't his name be cleared? Doesn't his son have the right to know if his father was a decent man?

I've never been comfortable accepting the fact I was living with a child rapist and killer. I know the family is always the last to believe their son, husband, or father was a killer, and that's a good thing. But somewhere in all those assumptions and accusations, somewhere among all the evidence and fingerprints—the cops failed to ask me the simplest question. It's the first question the police always ask on TV, the thing everyone in America knows you need when you're accused of a crime.

An alibi.

No one ever asked if Ben had an alibi the night Jaqui Moreland went missing.

I'm sure I could call the police today, and they'd have a half-dozen witnesses who saw Ben in the area where Jaqui's body was found. But if that's true, it only proves how far the police are willing to go to perpetuate a fraud.

I was grieving and emotionally drained when all this was going on a few weeks ago. Between the Roy thing, the media circus, Ben's book revelation, the threatening phone call, the evidence, the cops and FBI—it never dawned on me to remember where I was the night Jaqui Moreland went missing. I mean, it was so long ago, and Ben was never a suspect, so I had no reason to think about whether or not he had an alibi for that night.

But I now remember that Ben was ill, and I sat up with him because we were trying to decide if he needed to go to the hospital. When he went to sleep, I did, too.

In a chair in the same room.

Yes, he could've got up, got dressed, and left the house without me knowing.

But I doubt it.

And even if he did, it doesn't matter because the police have always maintained Jaqui was abducted between ten p.m. and midnight.

And I sat up with Ben till one a.m.

So he didn't do it.

I can't prove it, of course, but that doesn't make Ben a killer.

I press a button on my cell phone. Patrick Aub answers. I tell him my story and he says, "You're right, they've got two witnesses. One saw him, one saw his car."

"It didn't happen, Pat. They're lying."

"Why would they lie?"

"I don't know. Maybe the police coached them."

"You've been watching too much TV."

"Maybe. But I'm going to call for an investigation."

"Why?"

"To clear Ben's name."

"It's been a long time since Jaqui went missing. No offense, Dani, but I can't remember what I had for breakfast, and that was three hours ago."

"Ben was sick three times in the seven years I've known him. Once was just before he died, once was the night Jaqui went missing. I'm not mistaken."

"When are you planning to announce all this?"

"I'm taping a TV interview next week for a special report. I'm going to tell them I don't buy the alibi, or the evidence."

He sighs. "You know I'll stick by you no matter what, right?"

"Thanks, Pat."

"But my bosses aren't going to like it."

"Tough shit."

Chapter 68

SIX HOURS AFTER speaking to Pat, Sophie says, "Remember Uncle Sal?"

I smile. "Things still going well at the deli?"

"He wants to meet you."

"What?"

"Don't worry, I'll be with you."

"No way I'm going to meet a mob guy! Period."

"It doesn't work that way, Dani."

"What do you mean?"

"If Uncle Sal wants to meet the Pope on December twenty-fifth, the Pope cancels Christmas."

I show her my frustrated look. "When is this meeting supposed to take place?"

"Four hours."

"Where?"

"Cincinnati."

"What? We'd have to leave this very minute."

"That must be why the limo's in the driveway."

I go to the dining room, peek through the curtain. Then look at Sophie. "I pick one woman in the whole world to be my best friend..."

"Give it a rest. Let's go."

Four hours later, two goons escort Sophie and me into Sal's social club. In the main hall we walk past an enormous box with a wide slot near the top that's covered with angels, painted, it appears, by five year olds.

"What's that?"

"Uncle Sal's charity. It's called The Mothers of Sicily."

I start to say something, but Sophie says, "Don't *even*."

The goons open the door, and Sal jumps up from behind his desk and greets Sophie warmly. Then he looks at me and grins.

"Now I get it!" he says, winking at Sophie. "I'd do her myself if I was gay!"

Sophie and I give him an odd look and he says, "Wait. That didn't come out right. But you know what I mean. She's gorgeous." He looks at me again. "You're gorgeous!"

"Hello, Mr. Bonadello," I say. "It's a pleasure to meet you."

"And manners, too!" he says. "It ain't grandchildren, but it ain't bad. You can bring her around anytime. Anyone has something to say about it, they deal with me."

"Thanks Uncle Sal," Sophie says.

To me he says, "Every Fourth of July we have a big picnic and pool party. You'll come, you'll wear a bikini, yes? Yowzer!"

"Uncle Sal," Sophie says, "You might remember Dani lost her husband recently."

"Shit. You're right. I knew that. It's one of the reasons we're here. Still, she's so...well, never mind."

"Go ahead," Sophie says. "Say it."

"It's just that aside from family, I only seen one woman in my life as pretty as you. But you don't want to meet her. Trust me on this."

Sophie says. "She's an assassin from Vegas."

"Hey," Sal says. "That's a rumor."

"Right."

He and Sophie talk about the family a few minutes, then he asks me some general questions to be polite. Eventually he gets to the reason for our meeting.

"You need to drop this business about the police."

"What business is that?"

"I hear things."

"Did Patrick Aub call you?"

He looks at Sophie. "Who's that?"

"A local cop."

"What's his last name?"

"Aub."

"What the hell kinda name is that?"

I say, "The world thinks my husband was a child killer and rapist. He wasn't. He was a decent man. I'm going to clear his name."

"No," Sal says. "You need to let this thing fade from the—whatcha call—public consciousness. It'll be better for all concerned."

"Why's that?" I say.

He looks at Sophie, then me. Then says, "What I'm about to say doesn't leave this room, *capisci?*"

We nod.

To Sophie he says, "I'd feel better if you waited outside."

"Not a chance, Uncle Sal."

"I try to keep you out of the family business."

"I know."

He waves his hand at me. "She'll probably tell you everything anyway."

"Of course."

He nods. "We know who killed the kid."

I lean forward. "Jaqui Moreland?"

"Yeah. Killer's name is Gray Halloran."

"Who's that?"

Sal's desk is completely free of clutter, save for family photos and an ancient-looking phone with buttons across the bottom. He presses one of the buttons and says, "Send her in."

Seconds later a goon opens the door and Carter Teague walks in.

Chapter 69

"HELLO, DANI," SHE says.

"Carter," I say, trying to act nonchalant.

Sal stands. "My niece, Sophie Alexander."

"The singer," Carter says.

Sophie and I exchange a glance. There are only two chairs in front of Sal's desk, but several more against the wall. All black leather with rollers. Sal scoots one across the carpet and offers Carter a seat.

Now that we're all comfy and looking at each other, he says, "Tell Dani what you told me."

Carter says, "The man you know as Roy Burroughs is actually Gray Halloran."

"Did he teach drama at Riverton College?" I say.

She looks at Sal. He nods.

"As a matter of fact, he did," she says.

"Whose idea was it to take the photos of me?"

"Mine. I saw it as a potential score."

"But I erased them."

"Yes. Shall I tell the story or would you rather keep interrupting?"

"Go ahead," I say.

"The reason you and the police couldn't catch Gray, he wasn't a pedophile. It was never about Jaqui being underage."

"What about his text message about her nipples being as hard as his erection?"

Carter frowns at my interruption, but says, "Gray followed that forum but never chatted on it, so those words were written by someone else. As for Jaqui, she was hot to be laid. When Gray read her public announcement about setting a date with one of the local boys on the forum, he traveled to the boy's house and intercepted her as she crept into his back yard. The rest, as they say—"

"You're telling me Roy Burroughs is *ManChild*?"

"That's right."

"That would have to be the biggest coincidence in the world."

"How so?"

"Ben said he hired Roy—Gray Halloran, I guess—to pretend to be his old college roommate."

"That's right. Where's the coincidence?"

"Out of all the people in the world, the one he chose to play Roy happened to be *Manchild*? I mean, come on! What're the odds?"

"Pretty high, actually. Think about it. Jaqui, Gray, and Ben all lived in Cincinnati."

"Fine. You've narrowed the coincidence to one million suspects."

"Half of which are women."

I roll my eyes. "So it's one-in-five hundred thousand."

"You think five hundred thousand men were sleeping with Dean Fitzgerald's wife?"

"I certainly hope not!" Sophie says.

Sal laughs out loud.

I'm not laughing. It was Dean Fitzgerald who fired Ben from Riverton College.

Carter says, "Gray was sleeping with Patty Fitzgerald. The Fitzgeralds live in Clayton Court, which happens to be—"

"A half mile from where they found Jaqui's body," I interrupt.

"It's also three blocks from the backyard where Jaqui was abducted."

"Your point?" I say.

"At that time, Gray owned a green MGB. The night Jaqui Moreland went missing, a green MGB was seen parked near the scene by one of the neighbors. There were fewer than twenty such cars licensed in Ohio, and eventually the police contacted Gray and searched his car. They found nothing, but when they asked if he had an alibi, Gray said he and Ben Davis had been working on a project together."

"Which was a lie."

"Yes. On the chance the police might check, Gray called Ben and asked him to confirm his alibi."

"Why would Ben do that?"

"He knew Gray was having an affair, but didn't know it was Patty until Gray explained why his car was parked near the scene. Gray said if Ben didn't corroborate his story, Patty would have to, and he'd lose his job and tenure. Of course, Ben would have loved to call Dean Fitzgerald and say, 'Thanks for firing me. By the way, your wife's sleeping with Gray Halloran!'"

But he didn't," I say.

This is the favor Ben told me about.

As if reading my mind, Carter says, "Ben agreed to provide the alibi, but as luck would have it, the cops never followed up. Still, Gray owed him a favor, because he got to keep his job."

"So when Ben needed someone to break the news about my identity, he chose Gray, because he owed Ben a favor."

"That's right. Of course Ben thought Gray slept with Patty that night. He had no reason to believe Gray killed Jaqui Moreland."

"So Ben had Gray play the role of his old roommate, and created a story that made it plausible how Roy could discover my true identity."

"Exactly. Gray had been trying to talk me into dating him. When he told me Ben offered him eight thousand dollars to reveal your identity, I told him he was missing out on the big money. Nude photos of you would be worth a million dollars after your story broke. So we started dating, and I pretended to enjoy it."

Sophie says, "You're quite the whore, aren't you!"

Sal says, "Tell her about Ben."

Carter says, "Gray killed your husband."

"*What?*"

"Gray heard the cold case guys were about to get involved. He still had the panties and photograph, so he decided to kill Ben and frame him for Jaqui's murder."

"How could you possibly know all this?"

Carter shrugs. "I'm the one who planted the evidence in your house."

Chapter 70

I COME OUT of my chair so fast no one can react. But Sal pulls my hands off Carter's throat before any real damage is inflicted.

"You're a—whatcha call—spitfire!" he says. "But you need to calm down."

"I don't *have* to calm down! This bitch framed my husband for murder!"

"Be grateful you're hearing the truth. I came very close to never letting you know these things. Now sit down."

Sophie moves her chair closer, puts her hand in mine. I take a few deep breaths and say, "What do you mean Gray killed Ben? How?"

"Ricin poison."

"I don't understand."

"Ricin poison is extracted from castor beans. A lethal dose in humans is the size of a single grain of salt. Gray had access to Riverton's laboratory, and knew what he was doing. When Gray and I went to your house to meet Ben, he put the ricin in Ben's coffee."

"When?"

"The day before Gray broke the news to the tabloids."

"Where was I?"

"How do I know? The gym? Your office? You tell me."

"Ben lived several days after that."

"Ricin takes two to four days to kill, depending on how old or healthy you are. The symptoms show up as a flu bug, or severe cold, and keep getting worse until the heart gives out."

I feel Sophie squeeze my hand. I also feel the tears spill from my eyes.

"What kind of monster *are* you? How could you *do* that to Ben?"

"I didn't know Ben, so I felt no loyalty there. And you pulled a gun on me at the hotel, so I felt no loyalty to you. At the time I didn't know you erased the photos, so I was simply protecting my investment. I agreed to walk around the house and plant the evidence while Gray and Ben talked."

"How did you get all those items in our house?"

"I had a large tote bag. Ben never paid any attention to it."

Sophie says, "Why admit all this now?"

Carter looks at Sal.

Sal says, "Roy poisoned Carter, same way he poisoned Ben."

Carter says, "I was lucky. He left me for dead in a hotel room, but the maid ignored the Do Not Disturb sign."

Sal chuckles. "She was determined to put a mint on the pillow."

I'm in no mood to chuckle. Neither is Sophie. She says, "I hope you suffered. How could you date a man who raped and killed a child?"

Carter shrugs. "I thought there might be money in it."

"I've got a better question," I say. "How did you get Ben's fingerprints on that disgusting photograph?"

"I didn't. The police or FBI did that."

"That settles it. I'm going on national TV to demand a formal investigation."

"There's no evidence," Sal says.

"We've got Carter's testimony and my alibi for Ben."

"After today, there'll be no evidence Carter ever existed."

Sophie says, "What's going on here, Uncle Sal?"

"The truth? Gray got whacked."

"Why?"

"When Carter got poisoned, she contacted me through—whatcha call—intermediaries. I don't—whatcha call—condone child rape or murder. That can't go unpunished in my city. When I learned who did this terrible thing, I put the word out, and someone snuffed Halloran."

"So that's that?" I say.

"There's not much point in stirring up old bones."

"There is if the world thinks your husband's a child killer."

"That's your word against the cops. And they've got the evidence."

"I'll demand a formal investigation into the search conducted at my house when they found Ben's body. I'm a private investigator. I'll make it my life's mission to clear Ben's name. Plus, I've got the national media on my side. You can bet I'll find out who planted Ben's fingerprints on Jaqui's photograph!"

Sal says, "Let it go, Dani."

Sophie says, "She's not going to let it go. And I won't, either."

"Aw, shit," Sal says.

He sighs.

Then says, "Fine. Tell your story to the media. Let them conduct a—whatcha call—internal investigation."

"You think it won't work."

"I know it won't."

"Why?"

"The cops will never admit one of theirs planted evidence. Carter's getting a new face, new identity, and fingerprints. You could bump into her on the street next year, you'll never recognize her."

"What are you talking about?"

Sophie says, "The government. Uncle Sal got her a deal. The question is why?" She looks at her uncle. "Let me guess: Homeland Security? Fighting terrorism?"

He ignores her and looks at me. "I don't blame you for wanting to clear Ben's name. I like that about you."

I frown.

"I'm serious. I like you. I'm welcoming you to the family."

"It's not like we're married," Sophie says.

"But it's a good family, yes?" Sal says.

"It's a good family," Sophie agrees.

To me he says, "You're angry now. I get that. If I knew you were hiding out with my niece before Gray got whacked, I would've helped you clear your husband's sacred name."

I deepen my frown.

Sal says, "You're a spitfire. I like that. I know you're—whatcha call—annoyed with me at the moment, but I'm a good friend to have."

He produces a card with a phone number on it. No name, just a phone number. He pushes it across the desk to me.

"Someone bothers you? Call this number, *capisci?*"

"Thanks, Uncle Sal," Sophie says, on my behalf.

"Okay, then," Sal says. He stands. "So we're all on the same page about this?"

"Not really," I say.

"Why not?"

"I can't believe you're going to let this happen! Carter admitted her involvement, but you're going to let her *walk?* She could probably get immunity for her testimony."

Sal says, "Two problems with that. First, Halloran's dead. Second, Carter's deal has been made."

"But she could clear Ben's name. Think of his son."

Sal frowns. "I shouldn't have brought you here. I made things worse."

I stand and say, "You're refusing to help me?"

He looks at Sophie. "She's relentless!"

Sophie stands. "You should like that about her."

"I like *everything* about her. But she doesn't like *me*."

"I'd love to be friends with you and your family," I say. "But if you won't help me clear Ben's name, I don't see how that's possible."

Sal shrugs. "I can't help you, but I won't stand in your way. How's that?"

"Not good enough."

I turn to leave.

Sophie hugs him goodbye. Then she and I exit the social club, climb in the limo, and I collapse on her shoulder and start crying.

"Things will work out, Dani. We'll clear Ben's name."

"I know *that*," I say. "I'm crying about us."

"What do you mean?"

"I'm going to lose your friendship. And that breaks my heart."

I reach in my purse, pull out my cell phone, click a button, and hold it up so she can hear Sal say, "I can't help you, but I won't stand in your way. How's that?"

"You recorded our conversation?"

"I did. Everything's on tape. I'm sorry, Sofe, but I owe it to Ben."

"You're aware this tape could send Sal to prison?"

"Please tell me he's got some judges in his pocket and the best legal representation money can buy."

"Of course he does. But don't you even care how this will make me look to my family?"

"He should've searched us. I can't believe a crime boss would let us walk into his private office without searching us! I simply took advantage of his oversight."

"It wasn't an oversight, Dani. He trusts me. You took advantage of that trust."

"Like I said, I knew this would come between us. And that breaks my heart."

I put the phone back in my purse. Then it dawns on me the limo is still parked in front of Sal's club.

"Why aren't we moving?" I ask.

Sophie smiles.

"You know I love you," she says.

"I hope so."

"Well, I have a confession to make."

Chapter 71

I'M SITTING IN a limo with my best friend in the world, Sophie Alexander, whose uncle happens to be the most powerful crime boss in America. The limo's not moving, and I've just admitted taping her uncle's conversation during which he claimed to have specific knowledge of a gangland hit on Gray Halloran.

The limo and driver are owned by Sophie's uncle, crime boss Sal Bonadello.

The limo's supposed to be taking Sophie and me back to Nashville.

But it's not moving.

Sophie says she loves me, but has a confession to make. As I watch her smiling at me I start wondering how well I really know this 29-year-old country singer and song-writer.

"What's the confession?" I ask.

She points to the social club, and I watch five men enter the front door.

I recognize one of them.

Epilogue

WHEN DANI AND SOPHIE leave the room, Carter says, "How did I do?"

"Not bad."

"You think Dani bought it?"

"Which part?"

"That Gray made the poison instead of me."

"Yeah, she bought it."

"Because I admitted the other things?"

"Right. That's what makes the story—whatcha call—plausible."

"You think she suspects I killed Gray?"

"Naw." Sal smiles. "That was a—whatcha call—stroke of genius, poisoning yourself with the ricin. Hell of an alibi."

"So I get the job?"

"Whacking the councilman? I gotta think about it."

"What's wrong?"

"I'm not sure you're up for it."

She frowns. "You still have doubts? After all this?"

"I haven't seen you kill anyone. So far it's just you claiming you killed Halloran. It ain't easy looking a person in the eye, taking his life. And it ain't easy hiding the evidence afterward."

"I looked Gray in the eyes before pushing him off the balcony. That ought to count. And I've still got enough ricin to do the councilman."

"Where?"

She laughs. "In my purse."

"You took the ricin how long before pushing him off the balcony?"

"Twenty-four hours."

"That took guts."

"So I get the job?"

"Maybe. Why'd you kill him?"

She shrugs. "He outlived his usefulness. Gray was a total fuckup. He let Dani erase the photos. He went rogue and warned her about going to the tabloids. He made up that stupid story about Ben having a fixation on Dani when she was fifteen. Again, not part of the plan. Not to mention the fact he was *ManChild*."

"He was a—whatcha call—loose cannon."

"Exactly."

Carter looks at him and flashes a warm smile.

"What?"

"I like the way you handle yourself, Sal. There's nothing I find sexier than a powerful man."

He smiles. "I like the way you handle yourself, too."

"Maybe you should handle me."

He laughs. "I'm old enough to be your father."

"Really?" she coos. "Then why am I so fucking hot for you?"

He looks at her. "The timing's all wrong. You're about to disappear for a long time."

"We don't have to fall in love."

He smiles. "True."

She stands, unbuttons her blouse. Then removes it and says, "I thought I should prove I'm not wearing a wire."

He says, "I might need more proof."

"Do I get to kill the councilman before I go undercover?"

Her fingers are poised to unhook her bra.

"Yeah."

"You promise?"

"Yeah."

"Fifty grand, right?"

"Half up front, half after."

She removes her bra, lifts her right breast, licks her nipple. Then says, "How about you?"

"You want me to lick the other one?"

She laughs. "I meant take off your clothes. But sure, you can lick it."

"How do I know you're not wearing a wire under your dress?"

She smiles, reaches behind her, unzips her skirt, steps out of it. Then says, "If you'll kindly give me the down payment, I'll take off my panties and make you the happiest man in Cincinnati."

He crosses the floor, pulls a painting off the wall, punches six digits into the safe's keypad. He removes five bundles of cash, hands them to her. She riffles through them, places them in her handbag.

"Pleasure doing business with you," she says, stepping out of her panties. Then puts her hands over her head and does a cute little dance. "What do you think? Not bad, huh?"

He chuckles, approvingly.

"Your turn," she says.

"To dance?"

She winks and says, "To prove you're not wearing a wire."

Sal unbuttons his shirt. She says, "What the *fuck*?"

"Actually, I *am* wearing a wire. Gentlemen?"

The door opens, and three detectives and two plainclothes cops walk in. Nashville police detective Marco Polomo looks at Carter and whistles. One of the local detectives says, "You can put your hands down now, Ms. Teague. To avoid further embarrassment, perhaps you'd like to get dressed before we cuff you and escort you to the station."

FIVE MINUTES EARLIER...

OUTSIDE IN THE limo, Sophie says, "My confession is Uncle Sal agreed to help you clear Ben's name."

"*What?*"

"Carter contacted Sal months ago, hoping to get a job as a hit woman. Of course, Sal claimed he was a legitimate businessman and knew nothing about such things. So Carter got involved with Gray, instead. When she heard you erased the photos she realized she was getting nothing for all the work she did. So one night she poisoned herself. The next night she pushed Gray off the balcony so it would look like a murder-suicide. But she never told the cops about Gray being *ManChild.*"

"Because it would implicate her."

"Right. While Carter was recuperating in the hospital, she called Sal and tried again to get a hit contract. She said if she killed Gray, the man she was dating, she could obviously kill a total stranger. When Sal said that wasn't enough to warrant a major contract, she confessed to framing Ben and making the poison that killed him."

"Sal told you all this?"

"Uh huh."

"Why didn't you tell me?"

"Uncle Sal said your honest reaction would help make Carter confess after we left."

"Why would she confess?"

"She's still trying to get the hit job. Uncle Sal planned to pay her for a phony hit, and get her to confess on tape to framing Ben and killing Gray. Since the detectives are moving in, I guess it worked."

The limo driver must have gotten a text or some other signal, because he puts the car in gear. When we're a block away, I turn around and look out the back window and see the detectives escorting Carter Teague from the building.

I turn back to face Sophie and say, "You talked Sal into doing this."

She smiles.

I kiss her cheek.

"*Seriously?*" she says, smiling. "That's all I get for helping you clear Ben's name?"

I look her in the eyes.

It's time.

I press a button on the arm rest and hold it down until the divider rises into place, completely blocking our driver's view.

FINAL THOUGHTS

DANI RIPPER NEVER published *The Little Girl Who Got Away*.

The book was formatted, the cover chosen, but when Janie Ramirez sent courtesy copies to selected reviewers, they were shocked and horrified. Instead of seeing it as an uplifting account of good triumphing over evil, the reviewers said the subject matter was far too sensitive, and would alienate the public.

Sophie agreed.

Dani might change her mind and release the book at a future date, but for now, she's placed the project on hold, accepting the opinions of those who believe some stories are better left untold.

One of Dani's fans has asked for and received space on Dani's website to launch a campaign to release the book. If you would like to add your support, please go to http://daniripper.wordpress.com and click YES.

If you agree that this type of book should never be released, please go to http://daniripper.wordpress.com and click NO.

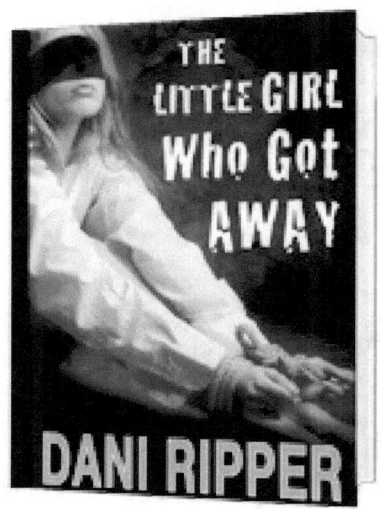

Synopsis for *The Little Girl Who Got Away*

Colin Tyler Hicks didn't have to work hard to capture 15-year-old Mindy Renee Whittaker and imprison her in the basement of his secluded farm house. But dealing with his manipulative young prisoner proves to be a formidable challenge for the creepy, schizophrenic killer-rapist. One of his personalities requires Mindy's death, the other requires her love. *The Little Girl Who Got Away* is the story of what happens when the plucky, resourceful Mindy refuses to become a sad statistic on a police report, and instead wages a life-or-death struggle against the powerful, psychotic killer-rapist, using only her wits and charm as weapons. This story is not for the faint of heart.

*   *   *

To see Dani Ripper's website and blog, go to: http://www.DaniRipper.Wordpress.com

To contact John Locke, or be placed on a mailing list to receive updates about new releases, click the "Contact Me" tab on his website: http://www.DonovanCreed.com

To follow John Locke's blog, go to: http://www.DonovanCreed.com

If you're a major fan of John Locke's work, and want to know what OOU means, go to this link and ask someone on the discussion thread: http://tinyurl.com/4mlbwzg

John Locke

New York Times Best Selling Author
#1 Best Selling Author on Amazon Kindle

Donovan Creed Series:
Lethal People
Lethal Experiment
Saving Rachel
Now & Then
Wish List
A Girl Like You
Vegas Moon
The Love You Crave
Maybe
Callie's Last Dance
Because We Can!

Emmett Love Series:
Follow the Stone
Don't Poke the Bear!
Emmett & Gentry
Goodbye, Enorma

Dani Ripper Series:
Call Me!
Promise You Won't Tell?
Teacher, Teacher

Dr. Gideon Box Series:
Bad Doctor
Box
Outside the Box

Other:
Kill Jill
Casting Call

Young Adult:
A Kiss for Luck (Kindle Only)

Non-Fiction:
How I Sold 1 Million eBooks in 5 Months!

www.ingramcontent.com/pod-product-compliance
Lightning Source LLC
Chambersburg PA
CBHW050923120626
46552CB00001B/11